GHOSTS OF ALCATRAZ

THE CLAIMING OF PATRICK DONNELLY

CAROL LYNNE

GHOSTS OF ALCATRAZ

THE CLAIMING OF PATRICK DONNELLY

CAROL LYNNE

WILDE
CITY
PRESS

WILDE CITY PRESS
www.wildecity.com

Ghosts of Alcatraz / The Claiming Of Patrick Donnelly
© 2015 Carol Lynne
Published in the US and Australia by Wilde City Press 2015

Published by Wilde City Press

ISBN: 978-1-925313-54-3

Cover Art © 2015 Wilde City Press

GHOSTS OF ALCATRAZ

CAROL LYNNE

PREFACE

The year is 2020 and the world is under a threat more dangerous than all the murderers and rapists combined. National treasuries are being depleted, military secrets stolen, and the global banking system is under constant attack. The threat of cybercrime has forced governments around the world to unite, forming the World Police Unit, or WPU. Deciding it best to keep the genius, but criminal, minds in one place, the countries involved reach a decision. Billions of dollars are spent rebuilding the one prison all men are afraid of…Alcatraz.

CHAPTER ONE

"Hello?" Jensen Black answered the phone.

"Warden, we've found another one."

"Shit. Call WPU. I'll be there in ten." Jensen threw off the covers and glanced at the clock. Three thirty. "Of course." He automatically touched the USMC flag he had attached to the bedroom wall as he headed to the bathroom.

He dressed and left his home. Located only three hundred yards from the newly remodeled prison, his home wasn't luxurious but it had an awesome commute. He crossed the courtyard and showed his credentials to the guards on duty. Stepping into the long corridor, Jensen looked from side to side. If the rooms weren't dark, he knew he'd be able to see the entire cell block in one glance. Made of two-inch-thick acrylic, every wall in the prison was see-through.

With Alcatraz now housing the most dangerous economic and cybercriminals in the world, governments refused to take chances. The prisoners were given absolutely no privacy at any time. The cells were transparent, and everything contained within those small ten-by-ten-foot walls of acrylic were the same, beds, toilets, sinks. It was no longer possible to hide even the smallest microchip. Each prisoner was given a single blanket and an inflatable, clear plastic pillow.

As he climbed the stairs to the guard station, Jeff, the guard in charge of the night watch, ran up to him. "Cell Block D this time."

"Prisoner?" Jensen asked, following Jeff at a fast clip. He absentmindedly reached to his front pocket for a cigarette. *Crap.* He pushed the craving down. What the hell had he been thinking trying to quit the nasty habit with all the shit that had been going down?

Jeff looked at the digital display in his hand and began reading the prisoner's stats. "Marvin Grimes, prisoner 1597832. Found guilty of draining more than a billion dollars from Germany's defense funds." Jeff tried to keep up with Jensen. "Sir? I think we should move the prisoners out of the immediate area until a cleaning crew can come in."

Jensen's steps faltered. This was the seventeenth prisoner found dead since Alcatraz had reopened its doors. They'd never before moved prisoners. Something in the guard's tone told Jensen Marvin Grimes's death wasn't like the others. "Why?"

Jeff wiped his mouth with the back of his hand. "I think you'll know once we get there. I was unable to get a visual on the prisoner."

More confused than ever, Jensen followed the guard down the stairs and took a left. The hallways were lit by underfloor lighting so the guards could do their jobs without disturbing the sleeping prisoners. Jeff unclipped the flashlight from his belt as they neared Grimes's cell.

Jensen took the flashlight from Jeff and pointed it into the acrylic box. No wonder Jeff hadn't made a visual on the body. The outer wall was covered from floor to ceiling in what appeared to be blood.

Swallowing the bile rising in his throat, Jensen stepped toward the cell next door and tried to see through the side wall. He was able to make out a few bits and pieces that he guessed were once the prisoner, but there was nothing that resembled a body. "Did you get an ETA from the WPU?"

"They're choppering in. Should be here any minute."

The World Police Unit had been the united governments' first line of defense. They, above all other law enforcement agencies, had been given global domain to track down and punish cybercriminals.

Jensen handed Jeff back the flashlight and left the area. "Do we have any empty cells?"

"A few."

"Move the prisoners immediately across and to the side of Grimes's cell. We'll curtain off the area if we need to, so the prisoners can't see the carnage." Jensen walked faster. He needed to get into his office before he made a fool of himself by throwing up in front of the guard.

* * * *

After reviewing the security footage once more, Jensen tossed his pen onto the desk and reached for a cinnamon disk. After unwrapping the cellophane he put the pacifier into his mouth. What the hell was going on in his prison? According to the scene he watched over and over again, Grimes had been sound asleep when he suddenly sat straight up and screamed. He appeared frightened, yelling at an unseen presence. Moments later Grimes's body jerked several times before turning back to the overhead camera, mounted above the acrylic ceiling. With a smile on his face, Grimes stopped screaming and began tearing his own body apart, opening veins with his bare hands. The first limb to be removed had been his left leg, quickly followed by the right.

Jensen knew it wasn't a matter of Grimes going crazy. No human could do to himself what prisoner 1597832 had done. Not only did the thin man not have the strength, but long after the blood had pumped from his body, Grimes continued to…disassemble himself, laughing maniacally.

The WPU suggested some kind of mind control, but Jensen had his own theories. He'd never been the kind of person to believe in supernatural stuff. Ghosts, possessions, hell, even tarot cards were things he thought were bullshit, but what else would explain what was happening within the walls of Alcatraz? No way could a man tear himself apart even under mind control. There was definitely something more sinister at play in the prison. He picked up the phone and called Fisher Marx. Fisher was not only his friend, but the man in charge of the WPU.

After several rings, the phone was picked up. "Marx," replied the deep gruff voice.

"Fisher, it's Jensen."

"I just got off the phone with Brandon," Fisher replied, not missing a beat. "He said you'd had another death, this one more gruesome than the others."

"Yeah, he wasn't exaggerating. Listen, I have a theory and I know you're going to think I've gone completely off the deep end, but hear me out."

"Okay."

Jensen began idly scribbling the names of the seventeen dead men on a sheet of paper as he continued to work through his theory. "Have you ever read anything about Alcatraz?"

"The specs. I had to approve the design."

"No. Not the new Alcatraz, the old Alcatraz. This place housed a huge number of cutthroat murderers. A lot of people died here in violent ways." Jensen closed his eyes. He couldn't believe what he was about to suggest to his friend and boss. "What if, when we gutted the prison, we disturbed a few of the lingering spirits?"

"Ghosts? Are you kidding me?"

Jensen sighed. "No. I know it sounds crazy, but so are these deaths. The prisoners are cybercriminals. Most of them were dragged out of their mom's basements, for Christ's sake. They aren't violent offenders. Yet every one of the deaths has been violent. I think we're dealing with something none of us are equipped to deal with."

"Spit it out, Jensen. What are you asking me for?"

"I want to bring in a parapsychologist," Jensen admitted.

"A ghost hunter? You can't be serious."

"I am. I'll stay out of the WPU's investigation, if you let me head up my own, using a parapsychologist." Jensen held his breath as the silence stretched.

"Dr. Brian Phipps."

"Excuse me?" Jensen questioned.

"If you really want to pursue this, there's only one man I'd trust, and that's Brian Phipps. I'll give him a call." Fisher cleared his throat. Jensen knew he was about to be issued a warning; it was classic Fisher. "If this gets out, the media will have a field day. As far as everyone else is concerned, Phipps is your longtime lover."

Despite that he was, and had always been, openly gay, the cover shocked him. "What? And I'm just supposed to traipse my lover around the prison?"

Fisher blew out an exasperated breath. "Hell, I don't know. Tell the guards he's an investigator. You don't have to go into specifics about the kinds of things he investigates. All I know is that I'll have a civilian in the prison that needs to be protected. Can you think of a safer place than by your side the entire time? If he's introduced as your lover, the guards won't question why he's staying in your house with you instead of in the dorms with them. He'll need to sleep in your house. I'm not kidding when I say this can't go any further than the three of us. I'd become a laughingstock, and you'd end up unemployed."

"Fine. Call Phipps. If he agrees, give him my number, and I'll work out the details." Jensen hung up and threw his pen across the room. Although being gay no longer carried the stigma it once did, having a lover move in with him would probably stir up the guards. He would definitely have to also give them a plausible reason why his lover was allowed on the island while theirs weren't.

Shit. He hadn't even considered what Dr. Phipps would think of the arrangement. Maybe all the worrying was needless. All Phipps had to do was say no to the ruse and Jensen would once again be up shit creek. Jensen shook his head. He couldn't control what Phipps agreed with or not. All he could do was come up with a reasonable explanation for the parapsychologist to be on the island.

Jensen picked up a different pen and resumed his scribbling, trying to come up with another good reason for Phipps to be given access to the entire prison. He could tell the guards Phipps was a security specialist, sent by WPU to live on the premises. If he did that, he wouldn't have to go the whole lover angle, but of course, that wouldn't explain why Phipps was living in the warden's house.

Jensen turned to his computer screen. "Computer. Photo of Dr. Brian Phipps, parapsychologist," he stated. The screen came alive with images of Phipps. "You've been a busy man," Jensen mumbled, reading various newspaper reports involving Phipps.

More than the array of cases the investigator had been involved in, Jensen was impressed by the image of the man himself. He looked similar to half the inmates Alcatraz housed—small, wiry, and smart. Jensen scanned through the photos until he reached a close-up. His cock stirred at the emerald green eyes staring back at him. Damn, he'd always had a thing for green eyes. The fact that Phipps's emerald beauties seemed to sparkle with untapped passion only made Jensen's cock harder. He pictured that small, compact body underneath him. Jensen groaned at the image of the two of them together. Their contrasting sizes would be hot as fuck.

The thought of one of the guards making advances on Phipps didn't set well with Jensen. Not only did he need to worry about the guards, but the damn inmates as well. Maybe pretending to be Phipps's lover wasn't such a bad idea. At least he'd be safe from unwanted advances.

Jensen chuckled. *Who the hell am I kidding? I want Phipps in my bed as much as anyone.* It had been months since he'd been to the mainland to scratch his particular brand of itch. First he needed to find out if Phipps even swung his way. If he did, Jensen had little doubt he could persuade Brian into his bed. Further research proved fruitful. Phipps was one of more than twenty percent of the male population who had come out of the closet once the world governments had passed their respective Equality for All Acts.

After entering his private restroom, Jensen surveyed himself in the mirror. He had a feeling Brian Phipps would be calling him on the video phone. It was something he'd do in Phipps's place had their positions been reversed.

Jensen combed his dark brown hair, noticing it was quickly becoming more gray than brown. At forty-two a man's hair may show his age, but his body didn't have to. After a twenty-year career in the military, Jensen still kept his body in prime condition. He studied his physique in the mirror. He didn't look like a bodybuilder by any means, but his muscle mass was definitely something he took pride in. He ran a hand over his rock-hard washboard abdomen. Did Phipps get off on muscles the way some of the men Jensen had been with did? Hell, did Phipps even like muscled guys like him, or was the parapsychologist into the more intellectual type of man? He thought about it for a few seconds and smiled. Yeah, just looking at his pictures, Jensen knew he was Phipps's kind of guy.

A beeping from his office caught his attention. With one last look at himself, he strode back to his desk and pressed the video monitor. The gorgeous thirty-three-year-old man appeared on screen. "Hello, Warden Black?"

Jensen grinned. "Call me Jensen, Dr. Phipps."

Phipps smiled, revealing deep dimples in both cheeks that hadn't shown up on the photos. Jensen noticed the seductive fan of Phipps's dark lashes as they swept playfully over his image on the screen. "I'll call you Jensen if you call me Brian."

"Deal." Jensen had a good feeling about this already. He'd been around enough to know when someone was sexually attracted to him, and by the way Brian was already looking at him, Jensen knew Phipps would be in his bed in a matter of hours.

"So, Fisher Marx said you'd come up with some sort of cover for me?"

Jensen hated to be the one to tell Phipps they'd need to pretend they were lovers. Why hadn't his old buddy at least taken care of that much?

"Yeah, but I'm not sure you're going to like it. The main thing is keeping you safe. The only way of assuring I can do that is by keeping you close to me while you're on the island." Jensen paused, trying to gather his thoughts.

"And?" Brian prompted.

"We need to be lovers."

"Excuse me?"

"Well, at least the guards and inmates need to think we're lovers," Jensen quickly added.

"And because we're lovers people won't question why I'm traipsing around the prison at all hours of the day and night?"

Jensen realized he hadn't spelled out the entire cover. He smacked his head with his hand. "No, sorry. We'll tell them I brought you in as a security specialist who happens to work for the WPU. As freaked-out as everyone is over the deaths, I think they'll welcome someone coming in to get to the bottom of the murders. The…uh…lover part is simply to keep you close to me and safe. Besides, I figured you'd want at least a little privacy to do your research."

Jensen watched as Brian began to chew on his lower lip. Jensen's cock hardened under the desk as his eyes zeroed in on the tortured lip. What did that plump little beauty taste like?

"And this is just for show, right?"

"Uh, yeah, sure." Jensen reached down and massaged his erection. *At least in the beginning.*

Brian exhaled and ran a hand through the silkiest-looking black curls Jensen had ever seen. "Okay."

Jensen wanted to pump his arms in the air. Instead he kneaded his cock once more. "I'll call Fisher and have your new credentials waiting for you at the tarmac."

Brian nodded and signed off.

Jensen sat back in his chair, the image of Brian burned into his brain. If nothing else, spending time around the man would be enough to fuel his jerk-off sessions for the next year or so.

* * * *

Jensen met the helicopter as it touched down. He'd already informed his staff of Brian's imminent arrival. They had grumbled until Jensen had informed them Brian wasn't just coming for a visit. When the guards heard the name Colonel Fisher Marx, they shut up immediately. To further provide cover, Fisher had suggested supplying Brian with false security credentials in the name of Brian Lassiter.

He wiped his hands on his slacks, suddenly nervous. What the hell? He was never nervous. Jensen reached for the pack of cigarettes in his pocket only to find it empty. *Shit.* Brian stepped out of the helicopter and Jensen swallowed around the lump in his throat. But then he'd never laid eyes on anyone as gorgeous as the man walking toward him. He briefly wondered if Brian smoked, and if he did, would he have extra cigarettes on him?

As soon as Brian was clear of the still-rotating blades, Jensen reached for him. He pulled Brian against his six-foot-four-inch frame and kissed him. Brian appeared surprised at first, but quickly got into character, so much so, that when Jensen thrust his tongue deep into Brian's mouth, the other man not only accepted the invasion, but moaned. Jensen could tell by the clean taste of Brian's mouth the man didn't smoke. *Damn.*

Jensen broke the kiss when he felt the need to thrust his cock against Brian. "Sorry about that," he whispered in Brian's ear. "Have to make it look good."

Brian looked up at him with heavy-lidded eyes. "I think you did a damn fine job."

Jensen smiled and wrapped an arm around Brian as he led him toward his house. He looked over his shoulder at one of the guards. "Please see that Mr. Lassiter's luggage and equipment are brought to my house."

"Yes, Warden."

As they entered Jensen's living room, he reluctantly released his hold on Brian's waist. The man felt far too right in his arms. "Did Fisher supply you with your new credentials?"

Brian tapped his back pocket. "Sure did. If anyone bothers to look me up, they should get a long list of cases I've solved." Brian shrugged. "I can't say I'm comfortable with the whole thing, but I understand the need for secrecy."

"Are you hungry or would you prefer to go over the cases before we eat? Although I'll warn you, you may not have much of an appetite by the time we're finished."

Brian shrugged out of his suit jacket and tossed it onto a chair. "Business first," Brian said, rolling up the sleeves on his pale yellow dress shirt.

"Does that mean pleasure later?" Jensen asked with a wink.

Brian shrugged. "I'm not used to mixing business with pleasure, but something tells me this case is unlike anything I've ever been involved in." Brian gifted Jensen with another of those sexy grins. "Besides, I may need another taste of that cinnamon-flavored mouth of yours."

Jensen gestured to his home office located in an alcove of the living room. He'd already had another comfortable chair brought up, as well as a separate desk and computer. "I thought you could work from here. My office in the prison is much bigger, but I was afraid I wouldn't get much work done with you there to distract me."

Brian's eyes narrowed as he sat in the large black leather chair. "I'm very good at my job, Warden. There should be no reason to bug you with questions once I learn the facts of the case."

Jensen took a chance and ran a hand up Brian's thigh. "It's your body that'll distract me, not your questions."

Brian coughed, and spun his chair toward the computer, tucking his legs under the desk and out of reach. "Shall we get started?"

Wanting to scream in frustration, Jensen popped another cinnamon disk in his mouth. He turned his monitor toward Brian and scooted his chair closer to the smaller man. He wasn't used to being thwarted in his overtures. When he saw a man he wanted, he fucked him. It was as simple as that. Brian was quickly proving to be a challenge he hadn't foreseen.

After scanning his retina and fingerprint, Jensen's computer came online. "We'll need to set your security clearance as soon as Duncan comes in."

Jensen opened the crime scene files. "For now, I'll give you a brief rundown of a few of our more memorable murders in the last four months."

"Prisoner 1549803, Hans Huebner. He was our first victim. Found sealed within the acrylic box the prisoners sleep on. Hans suffocated to death. We could find no way the prisoner could've gotten inside. The box was airtight."

Jensen looked at the video on the screen. "The cameras move on tracks above the cells. There's approximately a thirty-second lag time before it reappears above a prisoner's bed. Within that thirty seconds, Huebner went from on top of his bed to inside it."

"So why didn't a guard reach him in time?" Brian asked.

Jensen shook his head. "Unless you know what actually happened, it's hard to tell Huebner's inside the box. The guard stations are on a second floor above the cells. There are four of them, one in each corner of the building, connected by a catwalk. The guard on duty didn't notice it while sitting in front of the security console. We found the prisoner like that the following morning. It wasn't until we watched the footage of the previous night that we saw the move."

Brian said nothing for a few moments, obviously making mental notes. "Okay. Next one?"

Jensen went through several more of the unexplained deaths. There had been one a week after the newly refurbished prison opened its doors. Of the seventeen deaths, eleven had been some form of strangulation/asphyxiation, three spontaneous combustions, two apparent suicides by banging their heads against the sink, and the self-dismemberment death.

Halfway through the cases, Brian found a pen and began scribbling notes. When Jensen finished, he shut down the horrible images on the screen. "There you have it. If the pattern continues, we should be safe until early next week."

Brian tapped his pen against the paper. "I'm not so sure."

Jensen leaned closer, took a peek at Brian's notes. "What makes you think that?"

Brian turned his head and gazed into Jensen's eyes. "Because this last murder's different than the others."

"Dead is dead."

Brian shook his head. "I need to do some serious research. Mind if I use your terminal?"

Jensen felt he'd been rebuffed. He was in charge of the prison, for fuck's sake. Didn't Brian feel he deserved an explanation? "First tell me what you suspect."

"Don't take it personally. I'm used to working alone and that's the way I prefer it. These deaths are not the same. Yes, dead is dead, but the killers are very different."

"Killers?"

Brian tossed his pen onto the desk and scrubbed his hands over his face. "Let's just say you were right to call me in." Brian looked over his shoulder toward the kitchen. "I don't suppose I could get you to make me a sandwich or something?"

With his fears confirmed, Jensen stood and placed a hand on Brian's shoulder. "Yeah. I'll make dinner if you'll fill me in while we eat."

CHAPTER TWO

Brian ate a bite of spaghetti. He'd refused to look Jensen in the eyes since being summoned to the dinner table. It wasn't that he didn't enjoy looking at the gorgeous man. Brian simply had other things on his mind and didn't want to become distracted by the obvious sexual chemistry between them. From what he'd seen so far, he'd need every ounce of concentration to take on the big bads haunting the prison, and he had plenty to distract him already without adding the sexy warden into the mix.

The deaths thus far were more than disturbing; they were downright frightening. Especially the last one. "Do you have schematics of both the old building and the refurbished one?"

"I'm sure I can find them in the archives. Why?" Jensen asked.

"I want to make an overlay of the two and plot where each of our victims were housed."

They quickly finished dinner and Jensen retreated to the computer as Brian cleaned the kitchen. He knew from what he'd read on The History of Alcatraz web site that no cell adjoined a perimeter wall, thus making it even more difficult for a prisoner to escape. He wondered if the new and improved Alcatraz had kept that philosophy during its design and construction. Although the outer walls of Alcatraz had been kept intact, Fisher had told him the inside had basically been gutted. So what was tying the spirits to the prison?

"Got it," Jensen said from the other room.

Brian dried his hands and tossed the towel to the counter. He joined Jensen in the alcove and looked at the terminal screen. "You've got both schematics?"

"Yeah." Jensen flipped from screen to screen.

"Mind trading seats?"

Jensen stood and Brian scooted over. He refused to comment on the brush of Jensen's hand against his ass. There would be plenty of time for play later. Right now he held the lives of over three hundred inmates in his hands.

After about five minutes of manipulation, he overlaid the two images, lining up the outer walls perfectly. The old interior was shown in blue while the new, in red. Fisher had been correct. Very little of the old Alcatraz still stood. "They've made a lot of changes," Brian remarked.

"Yeah," Jensen agreed. "We only have half as many cells. The WPU wanted to keep the inmates inside the one building, so they made room for everything else the prisoners would need to ride out their sentences."

"Okay. Read me the locations of the dead men's cells grouped in the order written on that paper."

As Jensen began working down the list, Brian color-coded the prisoners' locations according to how and where they were killed. When he was finished, he sat back and looked at the whole picture. "Doesn't make sense," he mumbled, more to himself than Jensen. He couldn't see a pattern like he'd hoped.

"If I blow this up to poster-size, do you have a printer large enough?" Brian inquired.

"In my office. We often use it for the classrooms here on the premises."

"Classrooms? What could you possibly teach some of the most gifted minds in the world that they don't already know?"

Jensen smiled. "Auto mechanics, plumbing, heating and refrigeration, just to name a few. They used to be housed in a separate building but now line the perimeters of the prison itself."

Brian was just about to ask when Jensen continued. "The prisoners with life sentences aren't eligible for the programs. For those released eventually, it's our job to see they're trained to make a living outside of the business world. Part of their parole agreement is that they never own, operate, or so much as look at another computer again."

Brian grinned. "Good luck with that one."

Jensen shrugged. "It's someone else's job to enforce the agreement of parole. My job is to take care of them while they're here and make sure they're equipped to reenter the workforce."

Jensen stood and gestured toward the door. "If we're going to my office, I might as well show you around Alcatraz."

Brian rolled down his sleeves and put his suit jacket back on before following Jensen out of the building. They walked hand in hand in order to keep up appearances. Brian didn't mind the charade a bit. He found comfort in the much larger hand gripping his. Maybe a little break from his normally celibate lifestyle wasn't such a bad thing? It might be nice to spend a few days in the other man's arms.

"Over there's the employee housing dorm," Jensen supplied, pointing farther down the hill.

They walked the short distance to the prison and Jensen turned to Brian. "Do you have the security clearance card Fisher gave you?"

"Yeah." Brian released Jensen's hand and dug the wallet out of his back pocket. He produced the card and handed it to one of the guards.

The guy seemed to stare at him longer than necessary and Jensen cleared his throat. "Mine," he growled at the guard and pulled Brian against his side.

The guy gave a devilish smile and shrugged. "Just looking, Warden. No harm done."

"He's to be given full access to the prison. Marx wants these mysterious deaths stopped, and he's brought Brian in to help with that." Without another word, Jensen led Brian into the prison.

As soon as he stepped inside, Brian's jaw dropped. "Damn." He'd never seen anything like it. The view to the other side of the building was almost dizzying, the way people appeared to be right on top of each other. An idea struck him. "Can you leave lights on at night?"

"We could, I guess. I'm not sure how the prisoners would sleep, though. Seems kind of cruel."

The simple statement reaffirmed Brian's first impression of Jensen. The man was good at his job, but he also seemed to genuinely care about his prisoners. "Sleeping masks?" Brian suggested.

Jensen chuckled. "You know of three hundred and eight sleeping masks I can have delivered in the next couple of hours?"

"No, but I bet you could get them by morning."

"So what about tonight?" Jensen asked.

Brian rubbed the back of his neck. "Your call."

As Jensen looked around the facility, he idly ran his hand up and down Brian's spine. Brian doubted the man even knew he was doing it, but Brian's cock sure did. When he'd gotten hard enough to embarrass himself, he stepped out of Jensen's reach.

"We'll let it go for the night," Jensen finally said.

Brian nodded his agreement and the two of them walked farther down the corridor. He couldn't get over the engineering involved in creating this new Alcatraz. He knew he'd go crazy living in a fishbowl every moment of every day. For each cell block, there appeared to be a large social room with acrylic tables, chairs and a lone big-screen television. The nature show on the screen stood out in stark contrast to the boring color palette of gray and black the prison was comprised of. "That's what it is."

"Huh?" Jensen asked, once again resting his hand on the small of Brian's back.

"There's no color. I wondered why everything seemed so depressing. It just dawned on me that other than the gray blankets, guard uniforms, and televisions, there are no colors anywhere. Is there a purpose for that?"

Jensen unlocked his office, which had floor to ceiling blinds, and walked inside. "I guess I never really thought about it. The walls and furnishings are obviously security related. The blankets are what the WPU provided as well as the gray jumpsuits."

Jensen tossed his keys onto the desk and accessed his terminal. He appeared deep in thought as the system scanned his retina. "Why didn't I notice that? I walk around this prison every day, so why didn't I notice the lack of color? I take pride in treating the inmates with a certain amount of respect, but evidently that didn't include their living conditions."

Brian didn't like seeing Jensen beat himself up over the lack of stimulus in the prisoners' environment. Despite not wanting to get emotionally involved with Jensen, the need to comfort the big man was strong. Brian approached the desk and placed a soft kiss on Jensen's lips. "Because you were too busy trying to keep the prison safe, but now that you realize it, maybe you can rectify it."

Jensen nodded. "What would you suggest?" Jensen asked, pulling Brian against him.

The hard press of Jensen's body against his was too tempting to resist. He told himself that it was possible to have sex with the man but still maintain an emotional distance. As he talked, Brian couldn't resist running his hands over the sculpted chest he felt under Jensen's dress shirt. "The best way to add color would be new blankets and uniforms. Maybe a different color for each block or something. You could always tell the WPU it was for security reasons. It's much easier to tell if a prisoner is in an area he's not supposed to be if he's wearing a specific color."

Jensen sat in his chair and pulled Brian into his lap. "I appreciate the suggestions, and I'll definitely act on as many of them as I can get Marx to sign off on."

Jensen kissed Brian's neck, licked at his earlobe. "Now have we finally talked enough about business to get to some pleasure?"

The warden began unbuttoning Brian's shirt. God help him, he wanted to forget about the deaths for the next hour, but his conscience wouldn't let him. He stilled Jensen's hands as they began plucking and squeezing his nipples. "Not here. Let's get what we came in here for and finish the tour." Feeling bold, Brian ran a hand over the erection trapped within Jensen's pants. "It's not that I haven't thought about it since the moment I saw you on the computer screen, but I need to at least try and keep my mind on the job. Gruesome deaths kinda take away from my desire for sex, but later, I promise."

Jensen moved his hand from Brian's chest to his cock. He ground the heel of his palm against Brian's erection, applying just enough pressure to have Brian close to begging for release. Jensen knew it too. He chuckled and gave Brian a kiss. "Definitely later."

Brian stood and looked at the computer screen. "Can you print that in color?"

"Yep." Jensen scooted his chair to the desk. He tapped a few places on the screen and a giant printer in the corner came to life.

Brian carefully rolled the blueprint and wrapped a rubber band around it. "Ready to finish the tour?"

Groaning, Jensen stood and adjusted his cock. "Guess so. The faster we get it over with, the quicker I can have my way with you."

Brian had just stepped into the hall when the hair on the back of his neck stood on end. He whirled around, looking in all directions. "Shit. I need to run back to your place and get something."

Jensen must've seen the distress in his expression. He reached out and ran his hands up Brian's arms. "You okay?"

"Yeah, but I felt something. Why don't you stay here in your office, and I'll be right back." Brian turned and ran down the hall. He pushed the door open and waved at the guard who'd leered at him earlier. "Forgot something."

He raced to Jensen's and found his big black trunk right inside the door. Kneeling beside the old leather trunk that had once belonged to his granddad back when he'd done this for a living, Brian pulled out the plastic case among the tools of the trade. Since then, scientists had agreed that none of the tools worked. Brian kept them and carried them to each job out of respect for his relative. Unlike his granddad, the only instrument Brian carried with him was a voice-activated recorder. After retrieving his pride and joy from the plastic case, he shut the trunk.

Before leaving the house, he put the small receiver in his ear and brushed his black hair down to cover the device. He started to cross the courtyard. The recorder shrieked in his ear just as he was struck on the forehead. Brian's head snapped back as he fell to the ground. He heard running feet seconds before two guards knelt beside him.

Stunned, Brian sat up and looked around. He spotted a small piece of concrete three feet away. He covered the bleeding wound on his head and pointed to the object. "Can you hand me that?"

One of the guards retrieved the rock, handling it gently. "Is this what hit you?"

Brian took the piece of concrete. There was blood on one of the protruding bits. "Looks like it." Brian gazed at the location the rock had to have come from. "Is that lighthouse still in use?"

The guards both looked in the direction Brian gestured. "No. They deemed it unsafe. They had the choice of rebuilding it to bring it up to code, but they decided it was cost prohibitive, so they cemented it shut."

Brian held out his hand. "Here, help me up." The guard who'd ogled him earlier was the first to grab his hand.

"By the way, my name's Tony." Tony gestured to the other guy standing next to him. "This is Lenny."

"Nice to meet you." Brian pulled his hand away from Tony and started toward the prison. "Do you have a doctor on the premises?"

"Yeah," Lenny answered.

Brian made it to Jensen's office and knocked on the door. When the door opened, Brian fell into the strong arms of the warden.

"What happened?"

"Something hurled a rock at me." Brian lowered his hand to look at the blood. He could tell the bleeding was slowing, which hopefully would save him from requiring stitches. "I need a towel and a doctor in that order." He let Jensen lead him to the leather sofa. Brian stretched out while Jensen retrieved the washcloth.

"Here." Jensen moved Brian's hand and replaced it with the cloth.

"Does it need stitches?"

"I don't think so, but let me call the doc," Jensen said.

While waiting for the warden to make the call, Brian dug the rock out of his pocket. He remembered back to grade school, when kids would throw rocks at him because he was a little different. His mom always told him it was their way of getting attention. Was that what was happening again?

Jensen hung up the phone and then sat on the sofa next to Brian's hip. "What's that?"

Brian opened his eyes and held up the rock. "This is what hit me. I think it was thrown from the lighthouse outside the door."

"Not possible. That's been cemented shut," Jensen informed him.

"Yeah. That's what Tony and Lenny told me. I believe it was one of our resident spirits trying to get my attention."

"What're you saying?" Jensen asked, looking worried.

"Either they don't want me here, or they don't want me to leave. My job is to figure out which and why."

Jensen's brows shot to his hairline. "You think a ghost threw that?"

"I more than think. I'm almost positive. I felt something when I stepped out of your office earlier. That's why I wanted my voice-activated recorder. It's the only tool I've found useful in these situations."

"What're you going to do with it?"

"Well, as soon as the doctor takes care of this cut, I'm going to walk every inch of this place."

"Not alone, you're not," Jensen barked, crossing his arms over his chest.

Brian grinned. As tough as Jensen tried to be, Brian could see the underlying fear. "Strength doesn't work on a spirit, Jensen."

Jensen shook his head. "I'm still not letting you traipse around unescorted."

Brian rolled his eyes. Thank God he liked Jensen or he might be offended at the macho attitude.

* * * *

"So how does this work, exactly?" Jensen asked, as they slowly made their way down the corridor.

Brian stopped and looked up at Jensen. "I'm not really sure. I've just always been able to feel them. If I open myself completely to their presence I can sometimes communicate with them, but that's a pretty dangerous thing to do, so I only do it in extreme circumstances."

"So like you're psychic or something?" Jensen suddenly wondered whether Brian could read his mind.

"Well, in a way, I guess, but I think everyone has the ability; it's whether or not you know how to tap into that portion of your brain. I was lucky. My granddad, Ben, did this for a living as well. He taught me everything he knew."

"So you can't read my mind?" Jensen asked just to make sure.

Brian grinned. "I don't need to read your mind. I can read your body."

Within seconds, Jensen's cock went from half-hard to completely pile-driving hard. He groaned his frustration. They were in the middle of an acrylic maze and he wanted nothing more than to slam Brian against a wall and fuck him senseless. He looked at his watch. "Lights out in twenty minutes."

Brian nodded his understanding. "Let's continue our tour until then. We'll have all night to *discuss* your body language."

Jensen led Brian into one of the teaching areas. It was bordered on two sides by the outer prison wall. "This is the HVAC, plumbing and electric training room."

Brian walked over and placed his hand on the concrete wall. Jensen watched as the smaller man slowly walked the perimeter of the two old walls, never releasing contact. At one point, Brian pulled his hand back as if it had been burned.

"You okay?" Jensen stepped to Brian's side and looked at his hand. Seeing the reddened flesh, Jensen grabbed Brian's wrist. "The wall did that?"

Brian shook his head. "Not the wall. I need to look at the schematics I left in your office."

"Can we call it a night then?" He didn't like the idea of Brian continually putting himself in harm's way. Twice he'd been hurt and as far as Jensen was concerned, that was two times too many.

Jensen wrapped an arm around Brian as they returned to his office. He wasn't sure where this protective streak came from. It was out of character to say the least. He'd always been a rather selfish lover and he knew it. That, above all else, was the reason he'd never allowed himself to get embroiled in a relationship.

It wasn't hard to become self-absorbed when you'd grown up taking care of yourself. His mom hadn't been a bad woman, just incredibly busy. She had been forced to work two jobs to pay the bills, leaving Jensen to take care of himself at the age of six. He'd not been allowed out of the house except for school. The neighborhood he'd grown up in was more dangerous than the prison he now presided over.

Jensen had learned early to watch his back and take care of number one. That training followed him through twenty years of military duty and into his new job as warden. What was so different about Brian that he brought out Jensen's softer side this early in their acquaintance? Most of the men Jensen had been with in the past had been soldiers. Maybe it had something to do with Brian's overall size. At five-seven, and weighing maybe one hundred and thirty-five pounds, Brian definitely didn't have a soldier's physique, but Jensen could tell by the way he carried himself that the smaller man was in shape. Above everything, Jensen knew Brian had the heart of a lion; he had to in order to do his job.

They were almost to Jensen's office when Brian suddenly lurched forward, landing on his hands and knees. "What the fuck?" Jensen said, scooping the small man from the floor and into his arms.

"Let's get the schematics and get out of here for the night," Brian said, wiggling out of Jensen's hold.

Jensen unlocked his office door and quickly grabbed the roll of paper from his desk. He hurried Brian out the door and to his cottage. Once inside, he led Brian to the sofa. "Were you pushed or something?"

"Yeah. I just need to figure out why." Brian took the schematics from Jensen and started rolling them out on the coffee table.

"I think it's pretty obvious why they pushed you. Evidently they know what you are and don't want you in the building."

Brian shook his head. "I'm not so sure. I think they're merely trying to get and keep my attention. Believe me, if they really wanted me gone, they'd do something more serious than throw rocks, burn my hand, and push me to the floor."

Jensen studied Brian's profile, zeroing in on the bruise he could see underneath the butterfly bandage the doc had applied. "I don't think you should go back in. It's not worth the risk."

Brian shook his head. "That's not really an option at this point. They know I'm here. If I don't go back now, they'll do something even more deadly inside those walls to force me back inside."

Jensen couldn't stand it another minute. He pulled Brian into his arms and kissed him. As he tasted Brian's mouth, he vowed to protect the smaller man at all costs. "Come to bed with me?"

CHAPTER THREE

Brian glanced at the schematics on the table. He knew he needed to figure out what the spirits were trying to say, but it had been so long since a pair of strong arms had held him. He wouldn't be able to think clearly anyhow. He finally nodded and let Jensen lead him to the bedroom.

"Have you had your HIV shots?" Jensen asked on the way.

"Yes. My card's in my wallet if you need to see it."

"No, I trust you." Jensen closed the bedroom door and turned back to Brian. "May I?" he asked, hands poised at Brian's top shirt button.

"Only if we do each other," Brian returned. Jensen's grin was the only permission Brian needed. He slowly worked each button out of its hole, revealing the sculpted chest he'd seen earlier. Damn, how much exercising did this man do? Jensen's body was absolutely perfect. Brian loved the short patch of dark hair leading down to a thin treasure-trail that disappeared under the waist of Jensen's dress slacks.

He pushed the shirt from Jensen's shoulders, immediately attaching his lips to the tawny-colored nipple in front of him. As he sucked and licked the pebbled nub, Jensen removed Brian's shirt and started on his pants.

"You're so damn sexy," Jensen breathed in his ear as he slid Brian's zipper down.

Brian realized he was getting behind and quickly moved to rectify the situation. His hands fumbled with the fastener on Jensen's slacks as he continued to manipulate the nipple in his mouth. Some thought his obsession with nipples was strange. They always assumed if you were a breast man, you had to like women. Not so. To Brian, the size of the actual breast meant very little. He was more obsessed with the nipple, and Jensen had two of the most delightful ones he'd ever had the pleasure of sucking.

Jensen's hand surrounded Brian's cock and gave it several firm strokes. Brian released the nub between his lips and groaned. "That feels amazing."

He slid Jensen's zipper down, allowing the pants to fall to the ground. Brian ran his hands over the front of Jensen's underwear, relishing the feel of the prominent package still hidden within. Sinking to his knees, Brian slowly peeled the barrier down Jensen's muscled thighs.

The moan that escaped Brian was in homage to the beautiful cock bobbing in front of his face. It had been a long time since he'd tasted an uncut man. The dark red tip, dripping with pre-cum, peeked through the foreskin and dared Brian to take a sip.

With eyes fastened on Jensen, Brian grasped the long, thick shaft and peeled the foreskin back, exposing more of the tasty-looking head. He offered no teasing licks, instead opting to engulf the entire crown into his mouth.

Jensen's hands threaded through Brian's hair, holding tight. "Yessss," Jensen hissed.

Brian used his tongue to explore the heavily veined cock. He'd never been good at deep throating a cock the size of Jensen's, so he didn't bother trying, preferring to take his time on the head and the sensitive area just underneath.

One rather large vein caught his attention. Brian couldn't resist scraping his bottom teeth gently over the bulging skin. He grinned when he was rewarded with another groan from the bigger man. This was definitely hotter than anything he'd experienced in the last decade.

Fucking was nice and definitely had its advantages, but Brian had always preferred the foreplay that came before the rutting. He loved to work his partner up to a fever pitch, watch a man's eyes glaze over. That was power, and Brian relished it.

Brian felt Jensen's thighs tremble as he tried to hold himself back. No, that wouldn't do at all. He sucked the dick as deeply as he could and hummed a few bars of his favorite country song.

Jensen cried out as Brian felt the first volley of cum hit the back of his throat. He pulled off and directed the next shot to land on his closed lips before taking the head back inside to milk the remainder of the seed from Jensen's cock.

He loved the grunts Jensen unselfconsciously filled the room with. Brian knew he could get very used to giving Jensen pleasure. He didn't argue when Jensen reached down and lifted Brian into those heavily muscled arms. "That was...amazing," Jensen panted, licking cum from Brian's lips and chin.

Brian gave Jensen just enough of a shove to topple him onto the bed. He crawled on top of the bigger man and kissed him once again. Sliding his own erection against the hard six-pack of Jensen's abdomen, Brian moaned. "Touch me," he whispered.

He felt Jensen's hands smooth their way down his back before landing on his ass. Brian's tempo picked up as Jensen's fingers slid down the crack of his ass to tap against his sensitive hole. When Jensen applied more pressure and pushed the tip of his finger inside, Brian felt his balls draw up tight. "Fuck!" he yelled, moving to press his cock against Jensen's hip bone.

Three more thrusts and Brian jerked with his all-encompassing release, shooting burst after burst of seed between them. He collapsed, completely sated. "That was…wow."

Jensen chuckled and wrapped his arms around Brian. "I should've known you'd be a little hellcat in bed."

Brian lifted his head and looked into Jensen's gorgeous eyes. "Oh, you haven't seen anything yet. That was just a little something to take the edge off. Prepare yourself for round two."

* * * *

Brian watched Jensen sleep for several hours as he replayed the activities of his day over in his mind. Was it only twenty hours ago that he'd received the call from Fisher Marx? Brian shook his head. This had to be one of the longest days of his life.

He reached out and ran a fingertip around Jensen's nipple. He grinned as the small disk hardened. It had been obvious from their first kiss that Jensen was his kind of man, but Brian wondered how far he could allow himself to go. His job was too dangerous to fall in love. His granddad had repeatedly drummed that into his head.

Loving and living the kind of life he led didn't go hand in hand. Dealing with ghosts was a very dangerous profession. His granddad's philosophy even extended to his relationship with Brian. Although the older man cared for Brian, he rarely showed affection. He used to tell Brian it would hurt less when he was gone. Brian often wondered whether it was because of the pain his granddad felt at his wife's death.

Maybe he should concentrate on the case at hand instead of worrying about falling for a man who tasted like cinnamon candy. Brian gingerly lifted the covers and climbed out of bed. He picked his clothes up from the floor and carried them into the living room.

Dressed, Brian sat on the sofa and tried to concentrate on the schematic he'd printed earlier. With a cup of highlighters at hand, he plotted the murders, using different colors to denote the cause of death, the same way he had on the computer.

When he finished, Brian capped the pen and stared at the paper. "Pattern. What's the pattern?" he mumbled to himself.

Although the earlier deaths appeared to be in a rather crude line, the horrific dismemberment of Grimes didn't fit in with the rest at all. Brian glanced around the room. When he spotted what he was looking for, he rose and grabbed the magazine from the bar between the kitchen and living room. He settled back on the couch and spread out the magazine with the top edge placed on the first set of murders.

Yes! He'd been correct. The murders did form a line. He looked at the spaces in between the highlighted boxes that denoted prison cells. "Shit." Brian hastily rolled the schematic and practically ran to the bedroom.

"Jensen," he called, touching his new lover's hair. "I need to go next door."

Jensen mumbled something and rolled over. Knowing there was nothing his fierce protector could do anyway, Brian decided to let him sleep. He picked up his wallet on the way out.

After getting through security, Brian entered the prison. He climbed the stairs and stopped at the C Block guard station first. He rolled out the schematic and pointed toward several cubes. "Are these cells marked by number on the outside?" he asked the two guards.

"Where's Warden Black?" one of the men asked.

"Sleeping." He knew he needed to tell the guards something, but wasn't sure how much to divulge. "Look, I was brought in to help solve the mystery surrounding the recent deaths. You can either answer my question, or I can make a call to Fisher Marx."

There were a few seconds of grumbling as the men checked the monitors in front of them. "Yeah, they're marked."

Brian looked at the name tag on the man's uniform. "Okay, Joe, I'm going to need a flashlight, and then I'm going to walk the halls checking on these cells." Brian quickly made a list of the cell numbers. "Why don't the two of you concentrate on watching them over your monitors and from the catwalks?"

With the schematic tucked under his arm, Brian took off down the stairs. The hallways were lit well enough to see, so he saved his flashlight's batteries. After rounding a corner, Brian sank to his knees as a feeling that could only be described as evil passed through him. He retched violently, throwing up the contents of his stomach. *What the hell?*

Rarely was a spirit powerful enough to actually enter and exit a person. The movies made it seem commonplace, but the reality was much different. Most people didn't survive a possession. Brian's granddad was proof of that. He still didn't know exactly what kind of spirit had killed his granddad, but whatever it was had done so from the inside out. Brian shivered and wiped his mouth on his sleeve before cradling his spinning head. Was he being warned or played with?

After struggling to his feet, Brian made his way to the nearest restroom and splashed water on his face. He cupped his hand and managed to get enough liquid to rinse his mouth out. Brian grabbed a few paper towels to dry his hands as he studied his reflection in the mirror.

Suddenly, one of the toilets behind him flushed, sending a spray of blood into the air. Brian shielded his face as the overspray covered most of the small restroom. By the time the toilet died down, he, along with the room, was covered in blood. Fearing he would throw up again, Brian scrambled to clean his face and hands with another wad of towels.

He ran out of the restroom and straight to the security station. "What the hell happened to you?" the guard cried, running around the desk.

Brian swallowed around the bile creeping up his throat. "The bathroom. Blood." He shook his head, trying to clear it. It dawned on him the guard was alone. "Where's Joe?"

The guard pointed down the corridor. "Rounds. We do them every hour."

"I need you to call him and the warden. Get them both back here. I think we may have another death on our hands."

* * * *

Five minutes after getting the call, Jensen rushed through the doors. He didn't know what the hell had happened, but the guard on duty sounded shaken and mentioned something about the new guy being covered in blood.

The thought of that happening to anyone was enough to get Jensen's heart pounding, but the possibility that something had happened to Brian had set his nerves on fire.

The first thing he noticed upon entering the building was the lights. The fact that they were on was definitely not a good sign. He sprinted to the guard station and came to a stop. There, sitting in a chair, was Brian with his shirt off. His hair, areas of his neck and face, along with his pants and shoes, were covered in blood.

Jensen sank to his knees and cupped Brian's face. "Where are you hurt?"

Brian shook his head. "I'm not, but I think someone is. We need your help to find him."

"Wait, back up. How do you know someone's hurt?"

"I just do. I was in the bathroom and this happened," Brian said, gesturing to his clothing. "It shot up out of the toilet."

Jensen tried to wrap his mind around what Brian told him. He looked at Lance. "Where's Joe?" he asked, knowing Joe and Lance always had duty together.

Lance shrugged. "I tried to get him on his radio but so far nothing."

"Call the other stations. I want one guard from each to look for Joe."

As Lance called the other guards, Jensen returned his attention to Brian. "Why don't you go to my place and grab a shower? We'll take care of things here."

Brian shook his head. "It wasn't a coincidence that the toilet erupted in the restroom *I* happened to be in. They're sending me messages. I just have to figure out what the hell they're trying to tell me."

Reluctantly agreeing, Jensen stood and pulled Brian into his arms. "Let's at least get you cleaned up. We can use my private restroom."

"Okay, but only if we hurry."

Taking Brian by the hand, Jensen quickly led him to his office. Once in the bathroom, he found a washcloth and began cleaning the dried blood from Brian's face and neck. He had to distance himself a tad as he did so. The thought of actual human blood splattered all over the man he'd held in his arms earlier creeped him the fuck out.

"I don't understand any of this," he mumbled, unwrapping another candy.

"That's okay," Brian said. "I'm not sure I do either and I've done this kind of work almost my entire life. I've only run into tales of this kind of occurrence once before and it didn't end well for the parapsychologist." Brian watched Jensen toss the paper into the trash can. "What's with you and the candy?"

"Trying to quit smoking," Jensen grumbled. "Let's go."

Jensen hadn't missed the way Brian's voice changed when he spoke of the parapsychologist, but decided to wait and discuss it later when he could wrap Brian safely in his arms. He followed Brian back to the guards' station. The rest of the available men assembled and talked among themselves.

"Okay, Joe was making rounds. I want teams of two going over every square inch of this place until we find him." The men paired off and Jensen grabbed Brian's hand. "You're with me."

"Uh, sorry, guys, but if you run across a pile of vomit down the hall and to your left, it's mine, not Joe's," Brian admitted, eyes downcast.

Jensen noticed a few screwed-up faces at the image, but the guards dispersed without further comment.

"You were sick?" Jensen asked, leading Brian down the opposite hallway.

"Yeah." Brian shook his head. "It was the oddest thing. I was walking along the corridor and suddenly…shit, I don't even know how to describe it. It was like evil passed through me. It dropped me to my knees and I threw up."

"Why were you walking the halls this late at night anyway?"

As Brian filled Jensen in, he felt his hands sweat. "There's a pattern?"

"Kind of. Well, at least what I think is one. I'll show you the schematic later, but the murders look to be in a fairly straight line, all except the last. That one doesn't fit anything. Not the pattern, nor the cause of death."

The prisoners were pressed against the cell walls, peering out. Jensen tried to ignore their calls for answers, because he simply didn't have any at the moment. The men in his keep were becoming more and more agitated. Jensen knew he was going to have to do something before he had a riot on his hands.

He watched as one of the prisoners pounded his fist against the acrylic wall of his cell. "Calm down!" he yelled at the nerdy-looking man.

The man narrowed his eyes and punched the wall harder, leaving smears of blood on the otherwise spotless wall. "What the hell is going on around here, Brian? These men aren't violent offenders, but you'd never know that by the way they've been acting lately."

Brian walked up to the clear wall and seemed to stare directly into the man's eyes. "Who are you?" Brian asked the prisoner.

The prisoner laughed. The same maniacal laugh Jensen had heard on Grimes's tape. "Shit. Is he possessed?"

Brian's head tilted to the side as he continued to stare into the prisoner's eyes. If Jensen hadn't seen it, he wouldn't have believed it, but the prisoner seemed to have Brian under some kind of spell.

"Brian!" Jensen screamed, yanking Brian away from the wall. He cupped Brian's face in his hands and kissed him. "Come on, baby, come back to me." Behind him, the prisoner began that laugh again and Brian finally blinked. "Brian?" Jensen gently said his lover's name again. "Are you with me?"

After a slight shake to his head, Brian nodded. "I need to do some research."

Just then, the radio clipped to Jensen's belt came to life. "Warden, we found what's left of Joe in the lunchroom."

Taking a deep breath, Jensen picked up the radio. "I'll be right there."

He put his hands on Brian's shoulders and squeezed. "I need to go. Would you like to go to my office to do some of your research?"

Brian shook his head. "I'll stay with you for the time being."

Jensen wanted nothing more than to kiss Brian but too many eyes were on them. He turned to look at the prisoner, realizing the cell had gone quiet. The inmate was sitting on his bed staring at his hand as if he didn't know how he'd managed to cut it. "I'll have the doctor check it out as soon as I can," he told the bewildered man.

The guy looked from his hand back up to Jensen and nodded dazedly. Keeping Brian close to his side, he walked to the lunchroom. "So, how many of these situations have you worked on?"

Brian tried to chuckle but it came out as an unnatural bark. "Well, I've worked a couple hundred jobs, but nothing like this. If I survive, this will become the jewel in my crown."

The words chilled Jensen. "You'll survive. Don't doubt that for a moment. I won't let you out of my sight until we figure out what the hell is going on around here."

"What've we got?" Jensen asked the group of guards standing right inside the room.

"We don't know," Lance said. "I mean, we know he's dead, but…"

"Okay, I'll take care of it." Jensen walked to the area the guard indicated. He found Joe in the corner of the room. At least he assumed it was Joe. "What the hell happened to him?" he asked Brian.

When Brian didn't answer, Jensen faced him. Brian had gone completely white, his eyes unfocused yet staring in the direction of the body.

"Brian? You okay?"

Brian licked his lips and cleared his throat. "If you test the blood on my clothes it'll match what once ran through this man's veins."

"How do you know that?" Jensen asked. "Have you seen a corpse like this before?"

Brian nodded. "My granddad's. The medical examiner couldn't figure out where his bodily fluids had gone. He didn't have a wound on him. Like Joe here, his body had simply shriveled."

Jensen knew Brian had had enough. He led him away from the body. "Call WPU and get them out here to deal with Joe's body. Tell them I want a full autopsy, and I want two of you standing guard until they get here.

"Ready to go to my office?" Jensen asked Brian.

Brian shook his head. "I need to look at a few things in my granddad's trunk."

"Okay." Jensen led Brian toward the exit. "It'll be okay." He tried to soothe, kissing Brian's temple.

"No," Brian mumbled. "It'll never be okay again."

CHAPTER FOUR

"You need to get back over there," Brian said, as Jensen washed his back.

"I'm not leaving you here." Jensen spun Brian around and wrapped his arms around him.

Relishing the embrace, Brian rested his head on Jensen's chest as the warm water continued to rain over them. He didn't know why Jensen's arms felt so right after such a short amount of time, but he was sure it had something to do with their circumstances. "I'm safe here. Ghosts aren't known to haunt new buildings."

Jensen placed a kiss on the top of Brian's head. "The building may be new, but it was raised over the foundation of the first warden's home."

Brian closed his eyes and opened himself to his environment. "I don't feel anything besides you." He ran his hands down and rested them on Jensen's ass. "And you feel quite nice."

"I still wouldn't feel right about leaving you," Jensen said, reaching behind him to turn off the water.

"I'll be fine. I have some research I'd like to do, and you really should be there when the WPU shows up." *And I need to get my head back into the job before someone else winds up dead.*

Brian took the towel Jensen offered and patted him dry. Truth be told, he'd prefer to read his granddad's journal in seclusion. It was a chapter of his life he'd never come to terms with. Why he felt guilty over his mentor's death was obvious. He'd been a young man of twenty when it had happened. His granddad had called to ask for his assistance, and Brian had begged off because he'd had a hot date with someone whose name he no longer remembered.

"Brian?"

Brian glanced up, realizing he'd been lost in the past. "Sorry." He decided to just be honest with Jensen. "I need to go through my granddad's journal. I've never read it for personal reasons, but with tonight's death, I think it may hold a few clues about what's going on." He sighed and tossed the towel in the clothes hamper. "I think I need to do it alone."

Jensen's eyes narrowed. "You're sure? You're not just saying that to keep me from getting fired, are you?"

Brian shook his head. "No." He covered the distance between them and pulled Jensen's head down for a kiss. "I'll be here when you get home."

* * * *

After saying good-bye to Jensen, Brian opened the worn black trunk. He looked at all the antiquated tools of his granddad's trade, burrowed underneath them, and came out with the cracked leather binder.

Taking the journal to the sofa, Brian curled up in the corner and threw a blanket over his lap. He stared at the book in his hands for several moments before opening it. Brian couldn't depress the smile that blossomed at the old man's scrawl on the page. "You should've been a doctor, Gramps."

The journal was filled with cases his granddad had worked. As Brian continued to read, he became more and more engrossed in his mentor's storytelling, making his own notes and flagging pages with small scraps of paper.

Brian was so involved in his research, the kiss on his neck sent him off the couch and into a defensive stance. "Shit. You scared me," he panted, his hand going to his chest.

"I'm sorry," Jensen apologized. "I thought you'd heard me come in." Jensen walked around the sofa and sat beside Brian. "You okay?"

Brian nodded. "I think I found what we've been looking for."

Jensen scooted closer and wrapped an arm around Brian. Although it was a simple gesture, it warmed Brian immensely. "According to my granddad, he'd heard from another parapsychologist there was a nasty ghost killing patients at a century-old asylum. He took it upon himself to do some pretty extensive research about the place, and what he came up with was a type of ghost I've actually never heard of."

"How is that possible? You're one of the country's best parapsychologists."

Brian actually felt a blush rising up his neck at the compliment. "Thanks." He shook off the warm feeling to get back to business. "Probably the reason I haven't come across one of these particular bad guys is because it seems to be ghost lore. Few hunters have ever actually engaged one, let alone tried to banish it back to hell."

"Back to hell? You mean it's not the kind of spirit that usually haunts old houses and stuff?"

"Right." He flipped to one of the marked pages in the journal. "According to Gramps, there are several types of spirits, or what we call ghosts. Those that don't really know they're dead, and are therefore harmless, and those that seek retribution for their death. For the most part, I think we're dealing with the retribution kind of ghosts inside the prison. Then there are the truly evil spirits, called *Mundjis*. The Mundjis are ghosts that have basically escaped from hell. They actually feed on the evil of the second type of ghosts. That's why the Mundji we're dealing with is so powerful. He's feeding off the ghosts of Alcatraz."

Jensen sucked in a breath as he read the passage Brian's granddad had written. "So your granddad came face-to-face with one of these…Mundjis?"

Brian took the journal and closed it, then laid it on the coffee table. "I'm pretty sure he not only faced it but was killed by it." He felt his eyes burn as tears threatened. Knowing what he did, he couldn't believe he'd been selfish enough to blow his granddad off in his time of need.

"Hey," Jensen soothed, wiping the tears that had managed to escape from Brian's eyes. "What's wrong?"

Brian squeezed his eyes shut. The last thing he wanted was to pour his shame out on the table for Jensen to scrutinize, but the man deserved to know the truth. Brian still wasn't sure where their obvious attraction to each other would take them, but he'd have to tell Jensen eventually.

"I should've been with him the night he went up against the Mundji. Instead I let some closeted college jock fuck me."

Jensen didn't say anything right away, but Brian could've sworn he heard a deep growl reverberate in his chest. The thought of Jensen getting jealous over some nameless guy intrigued him.

Brian turned and straddled Jensen's lap. "You know what I need?"

Jensen grinned and thrust up against Brian's ass. "I'm hoping it's the same thing I need."

Brian chuckled. Despite the blood and death surrounding them, Jensen didn't let anything sidetrack him from what he wanted. Then again, maybe Jensen had the right idea. Brian knew ghosts weren't going to stop wreaking havoc anytime soon. Even if he managed to survive this job, there would always be another. Maybe taking a few minutes to appreciate life was just what he needed.

"Hey, where'd you go?" Jensen teased.

Brian blinked several times. "Nowhere. I'm right here." He ground his ass against Jensen's erection. *Fill me.* He'd never been with anyone who had the power to chase away the shadows. Despite his granddad's warnings, Brian wondered if Jensen would be the man he'd dreamed of his entire adult life.

Jensen pushed down the comfortable sweats Brian had put on after his shower. "Need you," Jensen whispered, taking a playful nip of Brian's earlobe.

Brian lifted his body enough for Jensen to get his sweats down and off, leaving his bare ass to rest against the heavy cotton of Jensen's pants. He sucked on the fingers Jensen presented, providing enough spit to ease Brian's passage.

"We could stop while I find some lube," Jensen offered.

Brian shook his head. He couldn't take the chance of the moment ending. He'd gladly suffer the bite of pain to feel every inch of the wonderful man in front of him. Brian released Jensen's fingers and held his breath as the sloppy wet digits found their way to his hole. "Yes," he groaned, when Jensen's middle finger breached the outer ring of muscles.

Brian braced his feet on the sofa cushions and fucked himself as Jensen added another finger. The stretch was unbelievable, but Brian needed more; he needed Jensen's cock. He needed to truly feel something with his heart and soul, even if it was just once before he died. He spat into his hand.

"Need it," he begged, unzipping Jensen's pants. Brian used the saliva in his hand to grease Jensen's erection, before moving it toward his ass. "Please." Jeez, since when had he begged someone to fuck him?

Answering Brian's pleas, Jensen removed his fingers and replaced them with the tip of his cock. "You're not quite stretched. It'll burn, ya know?"

"Don't care," Brian told him. He lowered his head to Jensen's shoulder. "Please don't make me ask again." *Please make me feel like I mean something to you.* How long had it been since he'd felt truly connected to someone? *Never.*

"I won't," Jensen assured him. "Take me whenever you're ready."

Jensen held his cock by the base, allowing Brian to slowly impale himself on the long, thick shaft. Jensen had been correct. It did burn, but not enough to make him stop. He welcomed the invasion, and continued down Jensen's cock until he was fully seated. With his eyes closed, Jensen showed no outward emotion, his face a mask of self-control. Brian grinned and leaned in for a scorching kiss, taking the time to nip and suck on Jensen's lower lip.

True to his word, Jensen didn't move. He ran his hands down Brian's back to cup the cheeks of his ass, waiting.

The second the burn gave way to pleasure, Brian opened his eyes and whispered, "Fuck me."

Those two little words unleashed Jensen's passion. He rolled to the side, putting Brian under him on the couch. With a devilish grin, Jensen withdrew his cock and surged back inside.

Oh, shit! Brian's skin broke out in gooseflesh as Jensen set a steady rhythm. He maneuvered his legs to drape over Jensen's shoulders, allowing the bigger man to plunge deeper. The new position put Brian's prostate in a direct line with the thick shaft filling him.

Letting himself drift to a place of peace, Brian relished the feeling of calm mixed with pleasure so intense he thought he might never recover. He began to spin a future with Jensen in his mind. It was the everyday aspects of normalcy that Brian longed for. He wanted simple things like coming home to someone after a long day, maybe planting a garden in the spring with a partner at his side or arguing over who left the cap off the toothpaste. He wanted a man, maybe Jensen, in his bed every night. Brian wondered if his longing to share a domestic existence with someone had something to do with his growing feelings for Jensen? Hell he couldn't even trust these strange new emotions. Maybe they had something to do with the stress he was under? Never having been in love, Brian wasn't sure what it felt like, and even if he did fall head over heels for Jensen, it could only lead to heartache for the warden.

"Gonna come," Jensen grunted, snapping Brian out of his daydream.

Brian reached between his legs and wrapped his hand around his cock. He knew he could come on a moment's notice, he was already that far gone. "Fill me," he moaned.

Jensen's entire body jerked, his eyes going wide as he drove deep one last time. Brian allowed himself to share the climax, shooting his seed between them. He released his cock and pulled Jensen into his arms, slipping his legs from the strong shoulders to wrap around Jensen's waist.

Brian rimmed Jensen's lips with his tongue before delving inside. He wanted to tell Jensen that he'd been dreaming of a future with him but said nothing. If something happened and the Mundji killed him, Brian didn't want Jensen to mourn him more than Brian knew he already would.

Jensen broke the kiss and gazed down into Brian's eyes, the emotion clearly written in his expression. The ringing phone startled them both.

Jensen pulled out of Brian's body. "Excuse me," he apologized, as he reached for the phone.

Brian released the breath he'd been holding and stood. He gestured to the bathroom and made his escape. Turning on the shower, he didn't bother waiting for the water to heat before climbing inside. Maybe he should tell Jensen how he felt and try to convince him to leave Alcatraz? Brian shook his head. No way would Jensen leave the prison without dealing with the current situation. Furthermore, Brian knew, despite his desire for normalcy, he couldn't walk away either.

The shower door slid open and Jensen stepped inside. "That was one of the guards on duty. He said the prisoners are demanding transfers."

"I don't blame them," Brian said, wrapping himself around Jensen. "Actually, I was going to suggest you do just that."

Jensen peppered several kisses to the bruise on Brian's forehead. "I'm not sure that Fisher Marx will allow it. The WPU is under scrutiny twenty-four seven from the international community. If we move the prisoners, the press'll get wind of it and wanna know why. It'll jeopardize everything. Billions of dollars have been spent on this facility. I doubt Fisher would so easily allow its name to tarnish."

"Try," Brian pleaded. "You've got over three hundred men who are sitting ducks for the ghosts. Can you live with another death knowing you could've prevented it?"

Jensen tilted Brian's chin up and placed a soft kiss on his lips. "I agree with you. I'm just saying I doubt the WPU will go for it, but I'll try, okay?"

"That's all I can ask," Brian agreed. He reached around Jensen and picked up the bottle of shower gel. After squirting a good dollop into his hand, he washed the muscular chest in front of him. After rinsing the soap from Jensen's skin, Brian indulged in his favorite body part. He attached his lips to Jensen's nipple and suckled greedily. The hardening cock pressed against his lower stomach was testament that he wasn't the only one enjoying the nipple play.

The phone once again rang, barely audible above the pounding warm water. Brian started to pull his lips from Jensen's pebbled nub, but Jensen's hand to the back of his head kept him in place. "I'll call them back in a minute. Don't stop."

Brian grinned around the nipple trapped between his teeth. He reached blindly for the bottle of gel and redirected the shower spray without removing his mouth from Jensen's chest.

The cool gel on his stomach made him shiver, but the skin of Jensen's cock rubbing itself against the soap warmed him. Oh yeah, he could easily get off with just this. Brian pressed his renewed erection against his lover's muscled thigh.

"I've never met anyone like you. It's fucking crazy, but I think I'm falling for you," Jensen whispered, his soapy hands finding their way to Brian's hole.

Brian squeezed his eyes shut. He wanted to tell Jensen he was falling as well. Instead, he released the now-bruised hard nub. "Please don't."

Instead of pulling away like Brian had expected, Jensen lifted him off the tiled floor. "Wrap your legs around my waist."

Brian did as instructed, glorying in the feel of Jensen's cock plunging into his ass. He thought their talk was over, but once fully impaled, Jensen spoke softly against Brian's lips. "Tell me why you don't want me to feel something for you?"

Brian swallowed around the lump in his throat. "If something happens to me…"

Jensen cut Brian's words off with a deep, tongue-tangling kiss. The kiss continued as Jensen continued to fuck him slow but hard. "I won't let anything happen to you," Jensen growled after releasing Brian's lips.

Brian sighed. He wished Jensen could do just that, but he knew reality didn't live up to dreams. "You won't be able to stop it."

"Then I hope it takes me as well, because I can't imagine living with myself if I let something on this island kill you."

Brian stilled. How could this wonderful man possibly care enough to willingly die for him? In that moment, Brian felt ashamed. What had he done to convince Jensen he was a better man than what he actually was?

Before he could respond, someone pounded on the door. "Warden!"

Jensen pulled out of Brian's ass and eased him to the ground. "What?" Jensen yelled, rinsing the soap off them both.

"We need you!" the voice on the other side of the door shouted.

"I'll be right there. Give me two minutes." Jensen turned off the shower and handed Brian a towel. They dried quickly and Jensen opened the door.

Brian was relieved the guard had already left the living quarters. "How'd he get in here anyway?" Brian asked, pulling on his sweats. He found a T-shirt in his duffel and pushed his feet into a pair of sneakers.

"That was Phil. He's my chief of security, so he has a key in case of emergencies."

Brian went to the front door and waited for Jensen to join him. "Good thing we weren't still on the sofa."

Jensen grinned and opened the door. "Good thing for Phil. I'd have had to kick his ass." Jensen tugged on Brian's hand. "Let's go."

CHAPTER FIVE

The noise inside the prison was deafening. Jensen's jaws clenched as he took in the scene around him. "What the hell's going on?" he asked.

Brian looked up at him. "I think it's a combination of things. The inmates are scared shitless. Some of them may be under a spirit's influence, and unless I'm mistaken, I'd say we have at least one more death on our hands." Brian pointed through the acrylic cubicles to one stained with crimson.

"Shit!" Jensen pulled his cell phone out of his pocket and punched in Fisher's number.

"Marx," the deep voice of his friend answered.

"Listen to this," Jensen said and held the phone in the air. After several seconds, he put it back to his ear. "We need to get the inmates out of here. I'm going to have them moved to the exercise yard for now, but you need to get them the hell off this rock!"

Fisher's breath was heavy in Jensen's ear as the head of the WPU hopefully came to terms with what they were up against. "Move 'em to the yard, but I can't promise anything."

Pissed with Fisher's noncommittal response, Jensen growled, "Let me take care of them, and I'll give you a call back." He shut his phone without waiting for a reply and turned to Phil. "Get all the outside lights on and start releasing these men to the exercise yard. Put live ammo in your guns and fire only one warning shot if things escalate. I'm not going to move these men to safety only to have them kill each other or try to escape."

Phil nodded and gazed around at the irate inmates. "We'll take the calmer ones out first. Maybe that'll clue in the others that their behavior will not be tolerated."

"Do what you need to do." Jensen watched Phil walk toward the security console and get on the phone to the other sectors of the prison. He grasped Brian's hand. "What'll we do about the ones who can't be calmed?"

Brian rubbed the back of his neck. "Get everyone else out first. When you're ready for the remaining inmates, give me a signal. I'll try and draw the ghosts to me while you whisk the prisoners out to the yard. Make sure they're as far away from the building as you can get them. Hopefully they'll be so busy with me they won't have time for schoolyard pranks like throwing stones."

Jensen's heart stuttered in his chest. "No. Think of something else." There was absolutely no way he'd let Brian draw all those spirits to him. He'd seen what just one of them could do to a man. The images of the dead inmates flashed before his eyes. "Definitely not."

Brian wrapped his arms around Jensen. "The amount of danger I'll be in will depend on how fast you and the guards move the prisoners. Once they're cleared, we all get the hell out." Brian pulled Jensen down for a kiss. The sweep of his lover's tongue only reminded him of what was at stake.

"I'll stay with you," Jensen offered.

Brian shook his head. "No. I told you, the biggest thing you can do to help me is get the men out. The ghosts can't enter me like they did the inmates. Yes, the ghosts can hurt me, but they can't do to me what they did to the others."

Jensen's eyes narrowed. This was the first he'd heard of this important detail. "Why can't they possess you?"

Brian grinned. "Something my granddad taught me. I drink about a quart of holy water every day."

"Seriously? And what, you just call up a local priest and have it delivered?" Jensen hated being flip, but Brian's explanation sounded odd.

Brian's head tilted to the side. "You must be Catholic."

Jensen sobered and shook his head. "No, why?"

Brian rolled his eyes. "The Catholics usually think they have the market cornered on all things holy. When in reality, anyone can make holy water. It's simply blessing the water in front of you. People all over the world bless their food before they eat, yet they think only a Catholic priest can bless a container of water." Brian shook his head. "Never made sense to me."

Jensen had never heard that particular belief but the more he thought about it, the more sense it made. "Okay. So you're saying your insides are holy because you drink this water, and therefore, the spirits can't possess you? So why don't we just have the inmates drink holy water, and why haven't you mentioned this tidbit before now?"

Jensen didn't miss the slight shifting of Brian's eyes to the side as he answered. "Didn't think it was important before now. Besides, you have to believe in the power of the holy water for it to work. We don't have time to bless the water and make every prisoner a believer. Just do me a favor and let me know when you're ready to move the rest of the prisoners."

Brian tried to pull away, but Jensen wrapped his arms even tighter around him. "You're not lying to me about this, are you?"

"No." Brian kissed Jensen, caressing his cheek as he kept the kiss going for several seconds. When he pulled back, he gazed into Jensen's eyes. "Thank you."

"For what?" Jensen probed.

"Making me feel whole for the first time in my life." Brian's eyelids flickered like he was surprised he said it.

Jensen watched Brian walk down the corridor, unease settling inside him. Why did that sound like a good-bye? Looking around, he decided to do what Brian had asked and get the inmates outside as quickly as possible. He'd deal with his feelings for Brian after they did their job.

* * * *

While Jensen and his men began removing the inmates, Brian sat against the far wall. He concentrated on his breathing, lulling himself into a pseudo trance.

He knew he'd been lucky to get away from Jensen earlier. It was obvious Jensen didn't quite believe what Brian had told him regarding the holy water. Truth was, Brian didn't really know if the water would keep the spirits at bay or not. He'd been honest about drinking it daily, but it was more out of habit than anything. His granddad was a man of strict routines and had drummed the importance of the daily dose into Brian's regime.

Brian silently prayed the chaos surrounding him would distract the big bad. He was fairly certain he could draw the second tier spirits away from the inmates, but he wasn't equipped to take on the Mundji.

He'd completely centered himself by the time he heard Jensen calling his name. With a deep cleansing breath, Brian stood and walked toward the back of the building, beckoning the ghosts to follow. As he opened himself further, he sensed the first stirrings of the spirits nearing. He felt like the Pied Piper as the ghosts swarmed toward him, licking at his heels. Brian prayed the ghosts would maintain their interest without resorting to violence until he was out of Jensen's eyesight.

The first slash to the back of his leg threatened to drop him, but Brian bit the inside of his cheek and kept going. Searing pain drew down his back as unseen claws raked the flesh from his bones. *Please hurry, my love.*

It wasn't simply the wounds that were painful. The constant barrage of spirits attempting to enter him were like battering rams against his soul. The men attached to the spirits may be long dead, but the heinous acts they committed in life still clung to their tainted souls. Brian stumbled to the floor, fighting to get away from the unseen talons that continued to tear his clothes and skin. He knew he couldn't outrun the vengeful ghosts, so it was time to try to reason with them. As wounds continued to open on his skin, Brian opened his mind. *If you kill me I won't be able to help you. I promise, I will find your graves and put you to rest.*

He'd barely had time to put the thought out before his world went dark.

* * * *

When the last of the inmates neared the door, Jensen turned to Phil. "Get everyone out. I have to find Brian."

Phil nodded and Jensen took off in the direction he'd last seen his lover. "Brian!" he shouted, sprinting the length of the long corridor. He rounded the corner and entered the woodshop area. "Brian!" he screamed, spotting the man he loved lying in a pool of blood. Brian's skin was flayed open, his clothes almost nonexistent as they lay on the floor in torn bits of fabric.

Jensen's military training kicked in. Without slowing, he scooped Brian into his arms and ran. *Why the fuck did I let him do that?* He pushed open the door and a cool breeze slapped him in the face. "Call for a helicopter," he shouted to the guards.

He ran to the gate and the guards let him through. Jensen didn't stop running until he made it to the cement landing pad. He lowered himself to the ground, still refusing to relinquish his hold on Brian.

"They're coming," he soothed, brushing Brian's unruly black curls away from his face. There were too many wounds to stem the flow of blood. He didn't know where to start, so he concentrated on talking, hoping like hell Brian could hear him.

"Come on, baby, show me those pretty eyes." He gently laid Brian on the ground and curled himself around the bleeding body. The shallow breaths Brian took gave him hope. The man was definitely a fighter. He'd seen men in the same physical condition as Brian simply give up, too tired to continue fighting for their own lives. How many young men had he watched die over the years? It was the reason he'd pulled himself off active duty.

Jensen heard the chopper in the distance. "Hear that? Help is on the way. Just hold on." He continued to talk to Brian as he watched the blood seep from his virtually lifeless body. "They'll fix you right up. They have to."

As the helicopter neared, Jensen found himself pouring out his heart and soul. "I thought I'd die never knowing what it felt like to really care for someone. In a matter of days you've given me more than anyone ever has. You may not say it, but when you look into my eyes, I can see that you're falling just as hard for me as I am for you. Don't give up on me now, baby. You just can't." Jensen's voice was thick with emotion as he tried to hold himself together.

The wind buffeted against them as the helicopter poised to land. Jensen leaned over Brian, shielding his lover from the flying bits of debris as the chopper touched down. He didn't move until a hand tugged on his shoulder.

"Let us in," a guy in a white uniform demanded.

Jensen scooted back far enough to let the medics have access to Brian, but refused to leave his side. He stroked Brian's cheek as he watched one of the guys start an IV.

"I'm going with you," he informed them, when they transferred Brian to a backboard.

"There's not enough room!" the man shouted over the sound of the chopper blades as they fired up.

The instant Brian was loaded into the chopper and Jensen's physical connection to the man was severed, his heart plummeted. Tears stung his eyes as they freely slid down his face. Before the helicopter lifted off, Jensen was dialing Fisher.

"Marx."

"Get me the hell off this rock and to whatever hospital they're taking Brian to!" he shouted.

"You need to wait until the inmates are evacuated. I've got several military transport copters headed your way."

"No," Jensen spat. "Brian's dying, and I'll be damned if I'll babysit a bunch of computer geeks."

"Among those *computer geeks* you'll find twenty-three that tried to financially bring down your own country, six who tried to arm US-held nuclear weapons, and an entire host of other international cyberthieves. You owe it to your country to make sure the transfer goes smoothly."

"I've done my time. I fought for the bureaucrats in Washington for twenty goddamn years. You want my resignation? You got it! Just get me the fuck out of here and to the hospital, or I'll call one of the local news stations. I'm sure I could get a transport from one of their helicopters."

"And face the wrath of the WPU legal department? I don't think so. You and I both know how nasty they can get when someone breaks their contract," Fisher said, his voice as cold as Jensen had ever heard.

Where had his friend gone? Jensen summoned all the patience he had left. "Please, Fisher. I'm begging you. The inmates are scared shitless. They're not going to give anyone trouble during transport out of here."

He was met by silence for several long, agonizing moments. "I'll send a boat. Be down at the dock in fifteen minutes."

"Thank you." Jensen started to hang up but Fisher wasn't finished.

"If something goes wrong, it's your head."

"If Brian dies, you can have it." Jensen closed the phone and stuffed it into his pocket.

He ran to his cottage. If he had fifteen minutes, he was going to use them to his advantage. He quickly changed out of the blood-soaked clothes and grabbed Brian's duffel. On his way out the door, he spotted the journal Brian had been reading. Jensen looked down at the book for several seconds before scooping it up and shoving it into Brian's bag. He glanced around the room, wondering if he'd ever be returning to his home. Although he'd only lived on Alcatraz a short while, it was more of a home than he'd known since he was a young kid, but being with Brian was more important. If that meant he'd never again step foot on Alcatraz, then so be it. He grabbed a bag for himself and left without bothering to lock the door.

He had just enough time to talk to Phil before he met the boat. He ran to the gate and tossed the bag to the ground. "Get me Phil," he told Lance.

"You coming in?" Lance asked.

"No. They're sending a boat to take me to the hospital. I just need to talk to Phil first."

Lance spoke into the radio clipped to his shoulder. "He'll be right over."

Jensen paced back and forth as he waited for his chief of security. "What's up?" Phil asked, coming to a stop on the other side of the fence from Jensen.

"WPU is sending military transports for the inmates. Once they're loaded, I want you guys to take off as well. Don't worry about going back to the dorms to get your stuff. Just get the hell off this rock, understand?"

Phil nodded. "What about you?"

"I'm headed for the hospital as soon as the boat gets here." He gazed deep into Phil's eyes. The tall, thick guard had been the closest thing he'd had to a friend on Alcatraz. "I hope you understand, but I've gotta go."

Phil nodded again. Phil was a man of few words, and Jensen was shocked by his friend's next statement. "If you need me for anything, you call me. You're the finest boss I've had, and I'll stand by you no matter what you're up against."

Jensen wished he could reach through the fence and shake his hand, but unless he wanted to be lit up like a

Christmas tree it wasn't going to happen. "Thank you. That means a lot to me."

He picked up the duffel and waved back to Phil as he headed down the rocky slope to the dock. As he stood looking across the water toward San Francisco, he shoved all thoughts of Alcatraz from his mind. Brian was the one who needed his strength now, not his job, not the inmates.

If Brian made it through, Jensen planned on taking him far away from California. He'd spend the rest of his life making sure Brian never had to endure that kind of torture again. As the first of the military transports landed, Jensen didn't even bother glancing over his shoulder. What he cared about was in front of him, not behind him.

CHAPTER SIX

By the time Jensen made it to the hospital an hour had gone by since he'd last laid eyes on Brian. Evidently, Fisher Marx had already made a few calls because as soon as Jensen told the woman at the emergency room desk his name, he was ushered to the trauma center.

"You can't go in the operating room," the nurse informed him.

"The hell I can't. Didn't Fisher Marx, head of the WPU, call?"

"Yes, but he only said to make sure you and Mr. Phipps were well taken care of."

Jensen pointed in the direction they were heading. "The best thing this hospital can do for both of us is to get me in that goddamned room."

The nurse stopped walking and crossed her arms. "Would you prefer to put him at risk of infection? If you'll please take a seat in the waiting room, we'll call you as soon as he's in recovery. He's under anesthesia anyway. He won't know you're there."

It wasn't like Jensen to give up without a fight, but the last thing he wanted was to put Brian in further danger.

He reluctantly agreed and was shown to the waiting room. Four hours and twelve cups of coffee later, Jensen was led to the recovery room after scrubbing his hands and putting a mask on.

Squatting down, he ran his hand through Brian's hair. "I'm here, baby."

Brian turned his head, tears streaming across the bridge of his nose to land on the sheet below. "Hurts," he gasped.

Jensen's gaze flicked to the doctor writing on a chart at the foot of Brian's bed. "Thank you," he said to the physician.

"He was lucky," the doctors said. "We had to pump almost four pints of blood into him."

Jensen closed his eyes and sent up a quick thank you to the man upstairs. He noticed the doctor kept glancing his way. Jensen knew the WPU had put the fear of God into the hospital staff. No way would anyone at the hospital question Brian's injuries, but the guy had to wonder what kind of animal had made the wounds on Brian's back and legs.

Jensen leaned closer. Despite the mask over his mouth, Jensen gave Brian a kiss on the cheek. "I love you."

Brian's eyes squeezed shut, more tears seeping out under his thick black lashes. When he opened them again, the dark green jewels looked into Jensen's soul. "I love you, too."

Sucking in a breath, Jensen tried to keep from sobbing. His nose burned as well as his eyes as he fought to keep the tears at bay. "No one's ever said those words to me before." What had he ever done in his lifetime to deserve such a gift?

"Then you must've surrounded yourself with idiots," Brian whispered, his voice giving out toward the end.

When Brian's lashes fluttered closed, Jensen looked up at the doctor again. "Will he be okay?"

The doctor lowered the clipboard. "His vitals are evening out. That's a good sign. He'll need to be watched for infection, monitored for pain. As far as long-term, he might need some physical therapy. Some of the muscles were torn. And I'd definitely advise he visit a plastic surgeon. The next few days will be critical though. If we can keep infection from setting in, he has a good chance of a full recovery."

Returning his attention to Brian, Jensen continued to pray. *Please don't take him away from me.*

It was another two hours before they finally had Brian settled into a room. Despite the pain meds they were giving him, Brian still whimpered occasionally in his sleep. Jensen sat by Brian's bedside, either holding his hand, or trying to soothe his lover with words.

"Once you get better, I'm gonna take you far away from here. I'm thinking a warm, tropical setting would suit you. Yeah, sandy beaches and palm trees. How does that sound? We can sit beside the ocean and drink those colorful fruity drinks all day. Then in the evening, I'll take you back to our little house and make love to you all night long, tell you over and over again how much I love you. Would you like that?"

Jensen noticed the more he talked, the calmer Brian seemed to be. He settled in his chair, prepared for a full night of dreaming up future plans for the two of them. He just hoped his voice lasted.

* * * *

The following morning, Brian tried to focus on his surroundings. *Why am I on my stomach?* He never slept in that position. He started to roll before he was fully awake. The searing pain stopped him, causing him to cry out.

A chair scraped against the floor and Jensen's handsome face filled his line of vision. "Where am I?" Brian asked, feeling nauseated and confused.

Before answering, Jensen kissed him. Brian tried to kiss back, but Jensen pulled away. "Hey, I wasn't finished. I need my cinnamon fix," Brian admonished.

"They let me finally take the mask off if I promised to be good. Besides, you need to conserve your energy." Jensen chuckled. "We both know that isn't going to happen if we start making out like a couple of teenagers." Jensen gently tugged on one of Brian's curls. "You're in the hospital. Do you remember anything about last night?"

Brian searched his mind. Flashes of the attack assailed him. His body flinched as he remembered the god-awful pain he'd endured, the voices screaming in his head to be set free and the memories of the men still attached to the spirits. "I have to go back."

"Like hell you are," Jensen rasped.

Brian tried to shake his head, but the pain lanced up his back again. "I promised them."

"Who? The spirits who tried their best to rip your body to shreds? Fuck 'em."

"You don't understand. I told them if they let me live I'd find their bones and set them free." Brian gazed into Jensen's eyes. "It's the right thing to do."

"What do you mean? You're going to find their bones?" Jensen asked.

"Judging by the number of ghosts that attacked me, I'd say there are around seven or eight skeletons still inside Alcatraz."

"Impossible," Jensen said, shaking his head. "Alcatraz was completely gutted. If there were bones, they would've been found."

Brian thought about the number of spirits who'd attacked him. How did the Mundji fit in? Had it always been in the prison or was it summoned by the spirits themselves to exact retribution? And how did the current inmate deaths figure into the puzzle?

"May I use your cell phone?" Brian asked Jensen.

Jensen shook his head. "You trying to get me killed? There're signs posted on every other wall about using cell phones in here." Jensen put the bedside phone within Brian's reach. "Can I ask?"

Brian grinned. "I thought I'd call an old friend of my granddad's. There has to be someone who knows more about the Mundji and how to vanquish it."

* * * *

After a rough day, Brian was finally asleep for the night. Jensen walked outside the hospital and called Fisher.

"It's about time," Fisher answered.

"Yeah, well, I've had my hands full. Did the inmates get transferred?" Jensen reached into his shirt pocket searching for a much-needed cigarette. *Shit.*

"Yeah. We had to house them in five different prisons, but they're all accounted for. We're keeping them out of the general population until they can be transferred back to Alcatraz."

Jensen shook his head in disgust and started across the street toward a convenience store. "The best thing that could happen to Alcatraz is a bomb blowing the place back to hell where it was conceived."

"You're talking about billions of dollars, Jensen."

"No, Fisher, I'm talking about saving lives."

As Fisher began to tell him the errors in his way of thinking, Jensen reached the store and stepped inside. Covering the phone, he asked the attendant for a pack of cigarettes and a lighter. After lighting up, Jensen inhaled the calming, body-killing smoke. "Brian's determined to go back inside," he confessed, taking another puff.

"Goddammit, Black, are you smoking?"

"Yeah, you gonna fly to California and stop me?"

Fisher sighed. "How's he doing?"

"Cut to hell, but determined to finish the job he was hired to do."

"He sounds like a damn good guy." Fisher cleared his throat. "I'm sorry he got hurt."

Something in Fisher's tone didn't sit right with Jensen. "You'd tell me if you knew something, right?"

"What're you talking about?"

"Brian said there're bodies still inside Alcatraz. That's why the spirits are there."

Fisher's lack of response was all Jensen needed to learn the truth. "Why didn't you tell me? We were friends."

"We still are. I gave you Phipps," Fisher responded.

"Go to hell! You set me up." Jensen tossed his cigarette to the pavement and ground it out with the toe of his shoe. "Brian could've died last night because we weren't given all the facts."

"That's bullshit and you know it. I'm sorry that Brian was hurt, but he knew damn well what he was getting into before last night. What he did, the risks he took, were his decision, not mine. I won't let you paint me with that brush."

"Where're the bodies, Fisher?" Jensen shook out another cigarette and lit up.

"I can't tell you that."

"Why? You've been my best friend for over twenty years. Don't you trust me?" Jensen continued to pace back and forth in front of the hospital. He couldn't think of a future without Fisher as his friend, but the betrayal cut deep.

"I've trusted you with my life on more than one occasion and you know it. But the information you're asking for is above your security clearance. I'm sorry. If I tell you, I'll be court-martialed."

Jensen closed his eyes. It was hard to imagine the one man who'd always been there for him turning his back when he needed Fisher the most. "I'm sorry, too." Jensen pushed the power button on his phone, shutting down any further conversation.

Jensen slid down the wall he rested against, throwing the cigarette into the street. He buried his face in his hands as his body began to shake with the emotions he'd kept at bay for over twenty-four hours. The man he loved was upstairs in a hospital bed pumped full of pain medication so he could sleep, and he'd just found out his best friend had betrayed him.

Getting himself under control wasn't easy, but Jensen was determined to pull himself together. Brian was a man of strong character, and he was determined to help the ghosts that had tried to kill him.

As much as Jensen wanted to put his foot down regarding the matter, he knew it would only drive Brian away. He even thought about lying to Brian by telling him the WPU had forbade anyone access to the island, but he quickly discarded that idea. Lying to the man he'd come to love wasn't something he thought he could do. He was left with little alternative other than accompanying Brian back to Alcatraz. Scared didn't begin to tap the emotions he felt about returning to the nightmare across the bay, but an hour spent away from Brian was even more frightening. He would protect Brian or die trying.

* * * *

A nurse taking his vitals woke Brian in the middle of the night. "Sorry," she whispered.

He nodded his head, fully aware the woman was only doing her job. "Can you make a note in my chart that I'm checking myself out in the morning?"

The nurse's eyes rounded. "It's far too soon for that, Mr. Phipps."

"Maybe," Brian allowed. "But I've been here for three days, and I'm leaving regardless. I just thought I'd give you a heads-up."

The nurse finished her tasks and left the room quietly. Brian turned to look at Jensen, sound asleep in the chair by the window. It was the fourth night Jensen had forgone a bed in order to stay with him. Each time Jensen came into the room, Brian could smell the cigarette smoke on Jensen's clothes. That more than anything told him something was bothering Jensen, but the stoic warden refused to talk. All Brian got was that Jensen had spoken to Fisher Marx and his old friend had been little help. Jensen had gone on to tell Brian he would be returning to Alcatraz with him.

Brian sighed, feeling guilty. Why should Jensen risk his life for a promise Brian had made? He studied Jensen's face while he slept. Was it possible Jensen was even more gorgeous asleep? "He loves me," Brian whispered to himself.

He remembered saying those words when he'd first opened his eyes in the hospital. Brian hadn't planned on telling Jensen. He thought it would save Jensen further heartache should something go wrong, but when he looked into Jensen's eyes, he knew nothing would save either of them should tragedy happen.

As he watched, Jensen's eyes opened. Brian grinned. "Sorry you're stuck with the chair again."

Jensen scooted closer to the bed. "How're you feeling?"

"A little stiff, but I'm okay," Brian answered, downplaying his pain. "I could use a kiss though."

Jensen obliged. Brian closed his eyes as the kiss went deeper. He knew it was more spiritual than physical; he could tell by the soft tongue that caressed the inside of his mouth. Jensen was demonstrating the depths of his feelings and it was working. Brian felt more cherished than he ever had. He knew in that moment he'd sacrifice anything for his man.

Brian began to doubt his resolve in returning to Alcatraz. Was he being selfish? *Definitely*. But he wanted a future with Jensen. His entire life he'd been trained to take over for his granddad. One of the rules of his chosen profession was *don't form attachments*. Brian had known better, but it'd happened anyway.

A commotion in the hall brought Brian's attention back. He pulled out of the kiss and looked into his lover's eyes. "Why don't you go see what's going on?"

Jensen kissed him once more and stood. "I'll be right back."

As soon as the door opened, the hair on the back of Brian's neck prickled. "Oh fuck." He tugged on the sheet covering him until it slid to the floor. Gritting his teeth as the hundreds of stitches in his back and legs pulled, Brian managed to stand and brace himself against the mattress.

He walked the four steps to the windowsill and picked up the pad of paper he'd written Emmett's number on earlier. He swallowed the rising bile, determined to work his way through the pain. After steadying himself against the bedside table, he picked up the phone.

"Hello?" a sleepy voice finally answered.

"It's Brian."

"I think I have a lead on someone who knows something about the Mundji," Emmett said.

"Great, but that's not why I called. I think at least one of the ghosts has followed me to the hospital. Is that possible?" Brian eyed the closed door nervously. "I mean, I know some spirits do that, but I didn't think I was dealing with a level one."

Emmett sighed. "When your young man called to tell me you'd been hurt, he said something about you promising the ghosts you'd help them."

"Yeah, I did. They would've killed me for sure if I hadn't made the promise."

"You've bound yourself to them." Emmett's voice broke. "I'm sorry."

Brian closed his eyes. "So you're saying if I don't fulfill my promise, they'll hunt me until I'm dead."

"You and everyone you come into contact with. They can be a persistent lot. I wouldn't fuck with 'em. Do what you have to do, but find those bodies."

"Thanks, Emmett." Brian ended the call. He didn't know Fisher Marx's number, so he grabbed Jensen's cell phone. With all the noise going on outside his door, Brian doubted a nurse would be in to yell at him. He scrolled through Jensen's contact list until he came to Marx's number.

"I'm surprised you called. After our last conversation, I doubted I'd ever hear from you again."

Brian didn't know what the hell Marx meant, but obviously the head of the WPU thought he was talking to Jensen. "It's Brian Phipps."

"What's happened to Jensen?" Marx's voice ratcheted up a notch.

"Nothing yet, but it will if you don't help me."

* * * *

The hallway was in chaos when Jensen stepped out of Brian's room. Nurses and doctors were wheeling crash carts in three different directions. "What's going on?" he asked one of the orderlies.

The guy didn't even slow down. Jensen followed the man, hoping for some answers. The room at the end of the hall teemed with activity. Jensen peered around the corner and came face-to-face with one of his biggest nightmares.

He couldn't determine whether the shape on the bed had been a man or woman. The white dry powder covering the form along with a fire extinguisher in the hands of a nurse told him all he needed to know. *Just like Alcatraz.* His heart skipped a beat. He'd left Brian alone.

Jensen turned on his heels and sprinted back to his lover's side, but was sidetracked by another team of hospital personnel as they rushed into the room next to Brian's.

One glance and Jensen panicked. He knew damn well what the scene really meant. *No! You can't have him,* he mentally screamed.

Machines beeped like crazy as a doctor attempted to cut the oxygen tube that had wound its way around the patient's neck. The guy was obviously already dead, his skin a deep shade of purple, his eyes almost popping out of their sockets.

Jensen threw open Brian's door and was surprised to see Brian on the phone. "We've got to get out of here!" he shouted as he moved toward Brian.

Brian hung up and gestured to his bag. "I agree. The longer I'm here, the more people will die. Grab the bag and let's go."

Jensen picked up the duffel and held his hand out to Brian. It was clear by the pallor of Brian's skin he was in a great deal of pain, but what was the alternative? If he tried to carry Brian, his stitches would only pull more, and staying in the room wasn't an option. "Can you make it?"

Brian bit his lip and nodded. "I don't have much choice."

"Lean on me if you need to. I don't wanna hurt you, so I'll leave it up to you."

They made it out of the hospital relatively easily. The staff were busy putting out fires and trying to save lives. By the time they reached the sidewalk, Brian had already thrown up from the pain. Jensen wished more than anything that he could pick his love up and carry him, but it wasn't possible. "Wait here and I'll try to hail a cab."

"No need. Marx should be pulling up any minute," Brian informed him, holding his stomach.

Jensen felt like he'd been punched in the gut. "What? You called Fisher? He won't help us. He already told me that. Besides, Fisher lives hours away by plane. He won't make it in time to help us."

Brian grimaced, his face screwed up in pain. "You just have to know what to say to the guy."

Before Jensen could question Brian, a big black car screeched to a halt in front of them. The window slid down and Jensen looked at the shiny bald head of the Ving Rhames look-alike inside. "Fisher," he greeted coldly, stunned that his old friend was in town. "What're you doing here?"

"Get in," Fisher's deep voice demanded.

Left with little choice, Jensen opened the back door and helped a near-naked Brian into the car. "Lie down on the seat, baby," Jensen instructed. "If you need to vomit, don't worry about getting Fisher's carpet nasty. It's a rental."

Fisher snorted from the front seat. "You're an ass, Black."

With Brian safely in the car, Jensen threw the bag on the floorboard and climbed into the passenger seat. Fisher sped away from the curb and glanced at his rearview mirror. "I've already rented a boat. It's waiting for us at the Gashouse Cove Marina."

Jensen was still confused. "Why're you doing this?"

Fisher reached between them and pulled out a file. "As of noon today, I'm no longer employed by the WPU."

"They fired you?" Jensen asked, taking the folder.

"I resigned. I left the letter on my desk last night after you called."

Jensen held up the file. "So what's this?"

"The end of my career and possibly the beginning of my incarceration," Fisher responded with a dry chuckle.

Jensen opened the folder and flinched. "Jesus Christ!"

"What?" Brian yelled from the backseat.

After looking at several of the graphic photos, Jensen passed them back to Brian. He tried to read the attached report, but the adrenaline flowing through his body wouldn't allow him to concentrate. "Talk to me, Fisher."

Fisher took a deep breath as he parked the car. "Let's wait until we get to the island." Without further explanation, Fisher opened his door and got out of the car.

Jensen looked over his shoulder. Brian stared at a black-and-white photo of a dismembered body. Brian met Jensen's gaze. "No wonder the ghosts are out for revenge."

Fisher pounded his fist on the hood of the car, making Jensen jump. "Come on!" Fisher yelled.

Jensen got out of the car and helped Brian before picking up the duffel. His gaze kept returning to the formidable island in front of them. "I sure as hell hope you know what you're doing," he mumbled to Brian.

CHAPTER SEVEN

Stepping into his house, Jensen no longer felt at home. Strange what a difference three and a half days and a couple of gruesome attacks could make. He took off Brian's hospital gown and helped him to the couch. Jensen glanced over his shoulder at a bug-eyed Fisher. He narrowed his gaze at his friend, clearly telling him to turn away from the sight of Brian's nude but tortured body. Fisher chuckled and walked into the kitchen.

"I'll get a sheet to cover you," Jensen told Brian.

"So how did you get to San Francisco so fast?" Jensen asked Fisher, as he pulled a pale yellow sheet out of the linen closet. He covered Brian, making sure the sheet tented over the back of the couch to keep from touching his mauled flesh.

Fisher came into the room and took up residence in Jensen's favorite chair. "I flew in during the night. I was asleep in the parking garage down the street from the hospital when Brian called me."

Jensen's gaze flew to Brian. "Why *did* you call him?"

Brian refused to make eye contact. "I knew you'd need him."

"And you will," Fisher butted in.

"Okay, so we're here. Talk." Jensen sat on the arm of the couch and reached down to idly stroke Brian's black curls, wrapping them around his fingers.

Fisher lifted the heavy file from the coffee table and flipped through it. He held up a picture. "This is Martin Williams, guard at Alcatraz from September 1947 to March tenth, 1963. On March tenth of 1962, Martin Williams was trapped in the prison library by nine prisoners. The door was barricaded and the inmates spent the next four hours raping and beating Williams.

"By the time prison officials forced their way inside the library, Williams was barely alive. The prisoners were sent to solitary and charged with rape, kidnapping, and attempted murder. Notice I said attempted murder. Williams somehow managed not only to survive the attack, but return to work seven months later."

"He came back?" Brian questioned.

Jensen could hear the tension in Brian's voice. He lowered his hand from Brian's hair to brush across the prickly whiskers of his lover's jaw.

"Yep. The psychologist in charge of treating Williams after the attack said his patient had come to terms with what had happened. He was actually the one who suggested Williams be sent back to Alcatraz instead of being transferred elsewhere.

"Williams was a career guard, so the officials trusted that his psychologist knew what the hell he was doing when he said Williams was ready to go back. After he returned to work, Williams continued performing his duties like a model employee until the one-year anniversary of his attack. The prisoners responsible for that attack were still in solitary. Williams bribed the guards and was handed the keys to the inmates' cells. Already disgusted by what the prisoners had done to one of their own, the guards left Williams alone in D Block."

Fisher placed the picture of Williams on the table and picked up several of the photos Jensen had seen earlier. "One by one, Williams entered the cells of his attackers, cut off their hands, raped them, and then proceeded to torture them—some by fire, some by strangulation, and three believed to be the masterminds behind the initial attack were found completely dismembered with a fire ax. After he'd killed the last one, Martin Williams put his service revolver into his mouth and blew his brains out."

"Fuck," Jensen mumbled. "I read everything I could get my hands on about this prison. So why did none of this turn up in my research?"

Fisher put the black-and-white pictures back into the folder. "Because government officials didn't want the general public to know. They closed Alcatraz down eleven days later, citing the reason as the building's deterioration."

"Wh-what did they do with the bodies?" Brian asked.

Fisher stood and tossed the file to the table. He put his hands deep into his pockets and walked toward the window. "Martin Williams's body was returned to his wife. The nine inmates were buried here on the island in one of the cellars."

Jensen was dumbfounded. How had the United States government gotten away with it for so long? "Where, exactly?"

"Doesn't matter. They're not there anymore. When plans began for reconstruction, the lighthouse was already deemed unsafe. It was decided to dig the bones up and encapsulate them within the structure."

"That's why the ghosts have suddenly surfaced. You disturbed them," Brian accused.

Jensen could tell by the rigid set to Fisher's shoulders and downturned head, his friend was ashamed of his part in the cover-up. "Why'd you go along with it?" he finally asked.

Fisher sighed and turned to face him. "It was already a fifty-year-old secret. I signed the classified agreement, not realizing it would come back to bite me in the ass, but when inmates started dying…"

"You offered up Brian to appease your own guilt," Jensen finished for his old friend.

"Yeah." Fisher's gaze swung to Brian. "I'm sorry. I had no idea things would get this bad."

Jensen rose from the arm of the couch and paced around the room. "So, the ghosts are the nine prisoners. What about the Mundji?"

"That's an easy one," Brian interjected. "Martin Williams was called back from hell by the spirits of the nine men."

"So how does a human become a Mundji rather than the other kind of ghosts we've been dealing with?"

"Because Williams was actually buried. His soul left this plane but instead of going to heaven, it went to hell, where it belonged. The nine inmates called a spirit directly from hell. That's a Mundji," Brian added.

"Why would they dredge up the ghost of the man who'd killed them in the first place? It just doesn't make sense to me," Jensen wondered aloud.

Brian looked from Fisher back to Jensen. "Because they're recreating the massacre the government tried to cover up."

* * * *

While Fisher took his turn swinging the sledgehammer, Jensen pulled another cigarette out of his pack and lit up.

"I can't believe you started smoking again," Fisher said with disgust.

"Yeah, well, stick around awhile and maybe the reason will hit ya," Jensen spat.

Fisher looked at him for several seconds before going back to work. The lighthouse doorway had been sealed with three layers of concrete blocks, making it difficult for even a man of Fisher's size to break through. Jensen wouldn't admit it to Fisher, but he still felt his old friend had betrayed him.

Jensen took another drag off his cigarette and stared at the house. He hated leaving Brian alone, but Brian had insisted on making his needed phone calls in private. Jensen looked down at the four big buckets of holy water Brian had prepared earlier. Brian had been emphatic that he be the one to administer the blessed liquid, saying Jensen still didn't believe enough in its power.

Fisher stopped swinging the hammer and took off his shirt. "This last one's a bitch."

Jensen studied Fisher. It had been a long time since he'd seen his friend without a shirt on. Despite his age, Fisher Marx was still one hot motherfucker. Marx had everything going for him—looks, job, power. Jensen still couldn't believe Fisher had given up the position he'd worked his entire adult life to attain.

"Why're you really doing this?" Jensen couldn't help asking.

Fisher wiped his face on his shirt and dropped to the ground beside Jensen. "Well, I could say because it's the right thing to do, but that's not the truth."

"So what is the truth?" Jensen prodded.

Fisher looked out over the foggy bay. "Because I love you, you stupid jerk. Nothing, not a job, not the threat of going to prison, nothing, is worth losing that."

Jensen was extremely touched. Years ago he and Fisher had played around a bit, but they decided they made better friends than lovers. Neither of them was interested in forming an attachment. Of course that didn't mean they hadn't counted on each other over the years for more than sex. Jensen put his hand on Fisher's massive shoulder. "I love you, too."

Fisher shrugged, dislodging Jensen's hand from its resting place. "Enough mush. It's your turn."

Smiling, Jensen stood and tossed his cigarette to the ground. "By the way, I'll give these up if we live through this."

"You'd better. I'm not saving your ass to have you die of lung cancer in ten years."

Chuckling, Jensen picked up the sledgehammer and went back to work.

* * * *

With trembling fingers, Brian replaced the receiver on its cradle. The conversation he'd just ended had shaken him to his core. How the hell was he supposed to defeat something as powerful as the Mundji?

He carefully got to his feet and grabbed the sheet of paper at his side. Brian still couldn't figure out why Miss Birdie Cox needed to speak with Jensen. She'd already informed Brian of the ritual needed to send the Mundji back to hell. What else could there be? *Maybe she needs to tell Jensen what to do once the Mundji possesses me? What if I'm not able to finish the ritual on my own?*

Slowly making his way outside, Brian called to Jensen. "Can I talk to you for a minute?"

Jensen stopped midswing and rushed to Brian's side. "What's wrong?"

Brian held out the sheet of paper. "I just finished talking to a woman Emmett put me in touch with. She's the only parapsychologist to ever take on a Mundji and survive."

Jensen's face paled at the statement. "And?"

"And she told me what I needed to do, but she also said it was imperative she spoke to you before we proceed."

Jensen took the paper and looked at the name and number. He glanced over his shoulder at Fisher. "Guess you're up, big guy. I've got a phone call to make." Turning to Brian, Jensen kissed him. "How're you feeling?"

"Sleepy. I know the pills are necessary, but they really knock me on my ass." Brian tried his best to smile for his worried lover.

"Why don't I get you into bed? We've still got a couple hours of pounding to do on that wall."

Brian held onto Jensen's arm, leaning on him as they walked back into the cottage and down the hall to the bedroom. "I'll rest for a little while, but I have to get things ready for later."

"You mean the ritual for the bones?"

"No, I mean the supplies needed to take care of the Mundji."

"Dare I ask?"

Brian momentarily buried his face into the pillow. He knew Jensen was going to have a fit, but there truly was no other way. In the end, Brian decided to tell Jensen only the basics. "The Mundji needs to be submerged in a combination of holy water and blood from the person he possesses," he confessed.

"The inmate bodies have all been removed from Alcatraz…" Jensen stopped as he realized what Brian was telling him. "No. Absolutely not."

"We don't have a choice," he tried to reason. "I'll pick a non-life-threatening cut to reopen, but it has to be my blood."

Jensen sat on the side of the bed and leaned down until he was nose to nose with Brian. "You expect me to sit by and let you bleed into a vat of water? Are you crazy?"

"No. I'm a realist." Brian reached up and cupped Jensen's cheek. "I want a future with you, and this is the only chance I have to get it." He pulled Jensen's head down for a kiss. "Hopefully by this time tomorrow we'll be able to walk away from all of this, together."

Jensen shut him up with a kiss of desperation. Brian was scared, but he'd do his best to soothe Jensen's fears. So when Brian broke the kiss, he grinned. "Go call Birdie, and I'll try to get some beauty sleep."

"I still don't like it," Jensen said, standing.

"I know, but think of the pot of gold at the end of the rainbow."

* * * *

Jensen wiped the tears from his eyes and walked outside. "I need to talk to you."

Fisher turned around, smiling. "Glad you're back. I think we've got a big enough hole to climb through."

Jensen waved Fisher off. "Leave it for a minute." He pulled a cigarette out of his nearly depleted pack.

Fisher dropped the sledgehammer and walked over to him. "Is there something wrong with Brian?"

Jensen shook his head. "I just got off the phone with the only person to ever successfully send a Mundji back to hell."

"And?"

Jensen squeezed his eyes shut, the tears falling once again. "In order to save Brian's life I have to betray him." The words still gutted him. It didn't matter that he had no intention of truly betraying his love; the fact that Brian would believe he had was bad enough.

"What're you talking about?"

Jensen stepped back and took a drag from his cigarette. "Birdie told me something that Brian left out of his explanation. The Mundji has to possess Brian before it can be vanquished."

"What about the holy water thing? I thought Brian said he couldn't be possessed."

"Holy water isn't what keeps the Mundji from possessing a person. It's the nature of his heart. A person needs to be filled with hate, which means I have to make sure Brian hates me in order to give this vanquishing thing a chance."

"Does Brian know?"

"Not that part, no. That's why Birdie asked that I call her." Stomping on his cigarette, Jensen glanced at the building. "I'm gonna need you to fuck me."

CHAPTER EIGHT

Brian awoke by a gentle hand on his shoulder. "Brian? Baby? We're ready for you to do your thing," Jensen said, placing kisses on Brian's forehead.

Brian loved opening his eyes to Jensen's gorgeous face. "When this is over, can we both go to bed and stay there for about a week?" he asked.

He noticed an expression on Jensen's face Brian couldn't identify. Moments later Jensen kissed him. "When this is over, we can do anything you want."

"Good to know," Brian answered. He held out his hand. "Help me up?"

Jensen nodded and eased him to a standing position. He held out a pair of dark green jogging shorts. "As much as I love your bits and pieces, I really don't think they need to dangle freely at a time like this."

Brian grinned and nodded his understanding. The pain that accompanied each movement threatened to send him to his knees, but he bit the inside of his cheek and bore it silently for Jensen's sake.

"There's no way you're going to lift those buckets of water," Jensen remarked, after getting the loose shorts settled low on Brian's hips. "Will it screw up anything if I hold them and you maybe sprinkle the shit around with a cup or something?"

Despite the pain, Brian couldn't help but chuckle. "You're the only person I know who'd dare refer to holy water as shit."

Jensen grinned. "Well, you know, I am one of a kind."

Brian tilted his chin up for a kiss. "You certainly are." Brian was grateful for the brief moment of normalcy, because what they were about to embark on was as far away from normal as a person could get.

After slipping on a pair of shoes, Jensen helped Brian outside to the old lighthouse. He was glad there was still plenty of daylight. He'd hate to think about going into the bowels of the oversized coffin at night.

He was surprised not to see Fisher. "Where'd Marx go?"

Jensen's face turned pink. "I forgot I was out of salt. Fisher went to find us some."

"In the prison?" Visions of Fisher's body being ripped apart by the already angry ghosts assaulted him.

"No," Jensen said, and kissed Brian's forehead. "He went to the guards' dormitory."

Brian blew out a long breath in relief. "You nearly gave me a heart attack."

Jensen took a step closer until Brian's body was flush against him. The kiss Jensen surprised him with was more passionate than any they'd shared in days. Brian actually felt his cock filling in the loose-fitting shorts. He groaned into Jensen's mouth as he sucked on his lover's tongue.

Breaking the kiss for some much-needed air, Brian gazed into Jensen's eyes. "I love you."

"I pray that you always do, no matter what," Jensen whispered against Brian's lips.

There it was again, that look. Brian couldn't help but to think something was going on with Jensen that he didn't know about. "Is everything okay?" he asked.

Jensen stared into Brian's eyes for several seconds. "Ask me that question when all this is behind us."

So, maybe that was it. Maybe Jensen was simply suffering from a case of nerves. "Okay," Brian agreed, dropping the subject. He caught sight of Fisher jogging toward them with two containers. "By the way, the salt isn't holy, so either you or Marx can spread that before I sprinkle the bones with the holy water."

"I'll let Fisher do it while I hold the buckets for you."

"Sounds like a plan. You ready to do this thing?" Brian asked, looking from Jensen to Fisher.

"No," Fisher said. "But let's do it anyway."

Brian waited for Jensen and Fisher to pick up the battery-operated lanterns already set out beside the newly created passageway. As he stood by the opening, he felt a chill race through his body that had nothing to do with the wind blowing off the bay. Movement off to his left caught his attention. Shadows swirled like small dust devils within the depths of the darkened lighthouse. "*I'm trying to help*," he broadcast. "*Just let me help you.*"

"Brian?"

Brian turned to see Jensen and Fisher standing behind him, supplies in hand. "You okay?" Jensen prodded.

"They're confused," he whispered. "I can't predict what they'll do." Brian looked over Jensen's shoulder at Fisher. "I'll understand if you don't wanna go in there."

Fisher shook his head. "It's my mess. I'll accept the consequences."

Brian nodded. "Let me go in first and calm them down."

"Be careful," Jensen said, then placed a quick kiss to Brian's lips.

Taking a deep calming breath, Brian entered the interior as Jensen held his lantern up through the passageway. It wasn't difficult to see the pile of bones dumped into a heap against the far, rounded wall. Brian was sickened by the total lack of respect paid to the murdered men. "I'm so sorry they did this to you."

Several of the discarded bones rose and flew toward Brian's head. He reacted quickly, blocking the majority of them with his forearm, feeling his freshly-stitched wounds pull. One, he believed it was an arm bone, clipped him high on the cheek. Brian winced, barely keeping himself from screaming. He could feel the blood slowly trickling from the gash toward his jaw.

Brian glanced over his shoulder to make sure Jensen hadn't seen. Luckily, he seemed to be too far inside the shadowed interior. The last thing he wanted was his lover storming in, upsetting the ghosts even more.

"Do you want me to help or not? I won't continue if you're going to hurl body parts at me." The air around him calmed somewhat. *"Thank you. I'm going to call the man I love in to help me finish this. Hurt one hair on his head, and I'll make sure you never get off Alcatraz. Got me?"*

Brian turned and called for Jensen and Fisher to come in. He wasn't sure where his bravado came from, but it seemed to calm the spirits more than his pleading had. As Jensen joined him, Brian pointed to the several bones that had been flung at him earlier. "Can you do me a favor and pick those up? They need to be returned to the pile."

Next he turned his gaze on Fisher. "Before we go any further, I think you owe these men an apology."

Fisher looked freaked-out. "Is that what they're demanding?"

"No, it's what I'm demanding. It doesn't matter what these men did fifty years ago, no one, and I mean no one, deserves to have their bones tossed into a pile and forgotten. It's absolutely despicable."

Fisher had the decency to look completely and utterly ashamed. "I didn't realize what I was signing off on. I'm sorry."

"Don't tell me, tell them." Brian pointed toward the remains.

Fisher did more than Brian ever expected when he walked over and knelt beside the pile and began to whisper. Brian couldn't hear what he said, but he knew it wasn't meant for his ears anyway. He also didn't miss the tears Fisher wiped away as he stood and turned back to them.

"What happened to your face?" Fisher asked, getting his first good look at Brian in the lantern light.

"Just a little misunderstanding. I'm fine." Brian looked at Jensen's worried expression. "Seriously, I'm fine." He gave Jensen a quick reassuring kiss. "Hold that bucket up for me, please. Fisher, can you liberally sprinkle the salt on the pile?"

As Fisher did what Brian had asked, Brian took a large cupful of the holy water. He'd learned long ago it wasn't a matter of praying over the bones, but rather sending them peaceful thoughts, urging them to cross over.

As he splattered cup after cup of water over the pile of bones, Brian talked to the ghosts. "There are people who've been waiting a very long time to see you. Please, leave this place and be with your loved ones. Your anger and the injustices done to you have been duly noted and will never be forgotten. Go in peace. Allow yourself the freedom of true death."

Once finished, Brian closed his eyes and opened himself to his surroundings. The immediate area around him appeared free of the restless ghosts. What disturbed him most was the thunderous evil still emanating from the prison itself. There was no doubt the Mundji was not happy its food source had crossed over.

Brian opened his eyes. "We'll sprinkle the remainder of the salt and holy water, but I think they're gone."

Jensen and Fisher sighed loudly. "How will we know for sure?" Jensen asked.

"We give these men a proper grave," he said, looking at Fisher. "When this is over, I need you to tell your ex-employers that they can either give these men what they deserve, or I'll go to the press. I also want a full pardon for any charges they may devise against the three of us."

Fisher nodded, and placed a strong hand on Brian's shoulder. "I'll tell them. Thank you."

Brian shook his head. "You did the right thing when it came down to it. I can't fault you for how you started the race, only that you had the heart to finish it."

* * * *

Jensen handed the television remote to Fisher. "I'm gonna hit the sack."

"I think I'll watch the news first. It'll be interesting to see what kind of spin the WPU put on the hospital deaths."

Jensen stood and stretched. His back popped as he worked the tension out of his spine. "Thanks for agreeing to stay the night. I just didn't think Brian was up to tackling the Mundji tonight after everything else he's been through today."

"No problem. It's not like I have a home to go back to anyway."

Jensen hadn't really thought of that. He was in the same boat as Fisher. "I guess we'll both be homeless after tomorrow, huh?" Jensen looked around his home. Other than his clothes and personal items, the rest of the furnishings had come with the appointed housing.

"I put a call in to an old buddy of ours from the service. Do you remember Conner Diggs?"

"Hell yeah, I remember Diggs. What's he up to nowadays?"

"He's a mayor, if you can believe it. A little town in southern Missouri."

"I'd have never guessed that in a million years. Diggs always seemed too rebellious to fit into polite society."

Fisher chuckled. "Well, I get the feeling Diggs isn't your typical mayor. Anyway, I asked him if he knew of any job openings in the police department down there."

Jensen almost choked. "Are you shittin' me? You wanna be a cop? You just retired as head of the biggest police force in the world. Why would you want to be a regular cop?"

Fisher shrugged. "Maybe to get the chance to do what I should've been doing all along, protecting people."

The lost expression on his oldest friend's face nearly broke his heart. Jensen sat down and wrapped an arm around Fisher. "Don't sell yourself short. You did a damn fine job of protecting people for the last twenty-three years."

"Yeah? Tell that to the seventeen dead inmates."

"Don't do that to yourself, man. You're gonna have to let it go or it'll eat you up inside." Jensen released Fisher and sat back. "So, a cop, huh?"

"Yeah." Fisher chuckled softly. "I could find out if Diggs could use one more good man on his force."

Laughing, Jensen stood. "I'll let ya know."

He waved good night and headed for bed. Stepping into the dark room, he tried to undress quietly so as not to wake Brian.

"It's about time you came to bed," Brian mumbled.

"Sorry, did I wake you?" Jensen eased onto the bed.

"No. I've been lying here thinking."

Sliding under the covers, Jensen scooted as close to Brian as he dared. "Something bothering you?" he asked, resting his head on Brian's pillow.

Brian didn't say anything but Jensen felt a tremor run through Brian's body. "Hey," he soothed, kissing Brian's cheek. "What's wrong?"

"I-I'm afraid. My granddad was a fantastic parapsychologist. If he couldn't beat the Mundji, what makes me think I can?"

Jensen ran his knuckles over Brian's five o'clock shadow. He hated to see him hurting. "Your granddad didn't have me by his side."

Brian buried his face in the pillow. "He didn't have me either." Brian's voice cracked as he confessed. "I should've been there with him. He asked for my help, but I blew him off to go out with some guy. Maybe he would've survived…"

"Shhh," Jensen soothed. "Don't think that way. We can't change the past." Jensen sighed. "I just had this same conversation with Fisher. What's with the two most important people in my life beating themselves up?"

Jensen snuggled closer to his man. "You know, as much as I love you, I really don't know that much about you. Like where do you live? What kind of childhood did you have? Do you have people in your life you can count on when times are hard? You know, the simple, everyday stuff."

Brian dried his eyes and turned his head to face Jensen. "Well, not much to tell, really. My mom had me when she was a sophomore in high school, so my grandparents adopted me. Mom graduated, moved across the country to Virginia with some guy. I talk to her maybe once a year, if that. Grandma passed away when I was eleven, and that's when I started hanging out with Granddad."

No wonder Brian felt so guilty about his granddad's death. It had just been the two of them for a long time. Jensen ran his fingers through Brian's hair. "So are you gonna tell me where you call home, or do I need to Google you?"

Brian chuckled. "Shall I give you the exact address, or will you be accompanying me back to Fort Collins, Colorado?"

"Fort Collins, huh?"

"Yep, I live in the same house where I was born and raised." Brian transferred his head to Jensen's shoulder. "So, you interested in moving to Fort Collins?"

Jensen curled his arm around Brian's head and played with his lover's earlobe. "It gets awfully cold there."

Brian ran his hand down Jensen's chest to grasp his burgeoning erection. "I've got blankets."

Jensen knew he should discourage Brian's advances. The last thing Brian needed was a rough-and-tumble with his wounds just starting to heal, but damn, did it feel good. He spread his legs and sighed. "Stop if it starts to hurt."

Brian scooted down a little farther and circled Jensen's areola with his tongue. "I can honestly say I doubt I'm up for fucking, but this I can definitely do." Brian latched on to Jensen's nipple.

"Feels so good," Jensen moaned. He repositioned enough to squeeze his arm between Brian's stomach and the mattress. Thank God his arms were long enough to reach Brian's cock.

When Jensen's hand encircled Brian's shaft, his lover automatically thrust into the hold. A hiss of pain escaped Brian at the movement. "Stay still. Let me do this for you," Jensen told Brian.

Although not nearly as thick as his own, Brian's cock was longer. It always seemed to work that way. It was the small guys who always got to carry around the biggest packages. "You gonna fuck me with this someday?" he asked.

Brian groaned and released Jensen's nipple. "Seriously? You'd let me make love to you?"

Jensen chuckled. "Don't let my size fool ya. I enjoy a cock in my ass on occasion, and this," Jensen said, squeezing Brian's cock, "would be a real pleasure."

Brian started jacking Jensen faster. Jensen's statement had obviously turned the smaller man on. He'd have to remember to talk dirty to Brian more often. Jensen heard a slight hitch in Brian's breathing as he continued to fondle his cock and balls. "You like that?" Jensen asked, picking up speed.

Brian answered by pushing his thumb against the slit on the crown of Jensen's cock. "Oh, I take that as a yes," Jensen panted, lifting his hips off the bed to fuck Brian's hand at an alarming speed. "You'd better catch up, or I'll be coming alone."

Jensen lifted his other hand and licked his fingers before easing them into Brian's ass. Brian gasped and stiffened when Jensen ran a finger over his lover's prostate. "Yeah, that's it, baby, give it to me."

The first string of heat to cover Jensen's fist tipped him over the edge. "Fuck!" he yelled as his balls emptied, completely covering Brian's hand in the thick white seed.

Pulling his fingers out of Brian's ass, Jensen kissed him. "I'll get a washcloth."

"Not yet," Brian mumbled. "I like the smell of our combined scents."

Jensen nodded and began licking Brian's cum from his fingers. He could definitely become addicted to Brian's taste. Jensen tried to imagine waking with Brian every morning. He prayed Brian would still want him after feeling betrayed. "You sure you don't mind me tagging along when you go home?"

Brian grinned without opening his eyes. "That depends. How do you feel about working in a bookstore a couple days a week?"

"Huh?" Jensen leaned up on one elbow and looked down at Brian.

Brian opened his eyes. "I own a bookstore. I'm always needing help."

That surprised Jensen. "I thought you did this ghost thing full-time."

Brian laughed. "There aren't that many ghosts around. Besides, except for travel expenses, I usually don't charge for my services."

"Well, I hope to hell you're charging the WPU."

"Yeah. I'd like to see their faces when they get my bill."

Jensen lay back down and teased Brian's lower lip with his teeth and tongue. "I never considered a career working in a bookstore. Are the benefits good?"

"Mmm-hmm," Brian hummed. "I hear the shop owner gives good head in the back room if you're lucky enough to get on his good side."

"Well, fuck! You're gonna have to fire the rest of your employees. I don't care if I have to work seven days a week."

Brian started laughing again. "I don't think you need to worry about Mrs. Halloran. She's sixty-three and the grandmother of eight."

"Yeah, I'll size her up once I meet her. If I see her looking at your basket, she's out of there," Jensen joked.

Brian chuckled around a yawn. Knowing they'd both need their strength, Jensen gave Brian one last kiss for the night. "Get some sleep."

"Mmm-hmm." Brian's breathing evened out and within a matter of moments he was sound asleep, blowing little puffs of air into Jensen's face.

Jensen tried to close his eyes and relax, but knowing what he'd be forced to do in a few hours kept sleep at bay. He was still awake when the sun rose the following morning.

CHAPTER NINE

Jensen placed the bowl of scrambled eggs on the table and sat down. "So, let's go through this once more. Fisher and I'll carry one of the inmate bunks into the library." He stopped talking and glanced at Brian. "You sure the library? Those beds are heavy as fuck."

Brian shrugged and put a forkful of eggs in his mouth. "Doesn't have to be, I guess. Just figured it was kind of symbolic, ya know, since he was attacked there and all." Brian's face flushed. "Hey, I've never done this before, don't forget."

Jensen reached across the table and put his hand over Brian's. "I know. So, you think it would work in a regular cell?"

Brian chewed his food, deep in thought. "Actually, I'm embarrassed to say, it might be a better plan." Brian looked from Fisher back to Jensen. "Once I get in there you could lock me in."

"No." Jensen shook his head. "Abso-fucking-lutely not."

Brian turned his hand over and threaded his fingers through Jensen's. "Once the Mundji is inside of me, I could very well kill you. Please don't put me through that. I'd never forgive—"

"I'll make sure," Fisher said, butting in.

Jensen looked at his old friend. "You'd help lock him in a cell?"

"If it'll keep you safe? I sure as hell would," Fisher stated with a nod.

Jensen threw up his hands in frustration and took his uneaten breakfast to the sink. "Forget I mentioned the cell. I'll get the damned bed to the library one way or another."

Brian shook his head. "No. I think since you mentioned it, the cell is a much better idea."

"Dammit, Brian! Why do you insist on making this more dangerous than it already is?"

Brian looked at him with understanding eyes. "If something goes wrong, nothing you could do would save me anyway. Please. At least let me protect you."

Jensen wondered if Brian would feel the need to protect him once he found him naked in the arms of Fisher. He knew in his heart what Birdie Cox had told him to do was wrong, but his head told him it was the best way to save Brian's life. The more hate in Brian's heart, even if it was directed at Jensen, the faster they could vanquish that evil son of a bitch Mundji back to hell. Yeah, his lover may hate his guts after all was said and done, but at least Brian would be alive. The more he thought about it, the queasier his stomach felt. "I'm gonna get the tools to cut the top off the bed." He stopped at the table and looked at Fisher, the man he'd be betraying Brian with. "You comin'?"

"In a minute. I'd like to finish my breakfast if you don't mind," Fisher answered, moments before shoveling another bite into his mouth.

"Suit yourself. I'm gonna grab the water hose and saw from the groundskeeper's shed. I'll meet you out front in ten minutes."

Brian watched Jensen until he disappeared out the front door. "He's mad," Brian mumbled, pushing his plate away.

"He's worried. There's a difference," Fisher replied.

"That makes two of us."

"No. That makes three of us." Fisher sighed, and scooped the last of the eggs onto his plate. "You're lucky, ya know?"

Lucky? That wasn't a word he'd have connected to himself at that moment. "Yeah, why?"

"Because Jensen loves you." Fisher studied his plate. "As far as I know, Jensen's never loved anyone."

Brian ran a hand through his hair. He knew that tone of voice, and the realization was like a blow to the stomach. "You love him," Brian finally said.

"Yeah. We had a thing for a while, feelings were definitely there on my part, but they've never been reciprocated. Despite everything that's happened between the two of us, I still love the jackass." Fisher stood and picked up his plate. "You finished?" Fisher asked, gesturing to Brian's plate.

"Yes. Thank you." Brian watched as Fisher took the dishes to the sink. He was still stunned by Fisher's confession. If Jensen could've had a man like that, why in the world would he want a scrawny parapsychologist?

The biggest shock was the fact the two men had obviously had an affair. He wondered why Jensen hadn't mentioned it. "Does Jensen know you love him?" he had to ask.

Fisher dried his hands on a towel and tossed it onto the counter. "Yeah. I told him again yesterday, as a matter of fact."

Brian swallowed, trying to force down the bile that rose up his esophagus. Before he could form a reply Fisher turned. "I'd better head over. He'll be pissed if he has to wait on me. You want us to call you once we get the top cut off the bed and get it filled with water?"

"Yeah," he finally answered. His mind was a million miles away. He heard the door open and close and buried his face in his hands. What if Fisher tried to take Jensen from him? The more he thought about it, the more depressed he became. Shit, maybe going off with Fisher would be the best thing for Jensen. At least Jensen wouldn't be under threat of ghosts and creatures pulled up from the bowels of hell.

What if Brian died during the vanquishing? How long would it take for Jensen to forget him and move on? Would Jensen seek comfort in Fisher's arms?

After spending a good thirty minutes worrying, he called Mrs. Halloran and checked on the store.

It was over an hour later when he hung up, still shaking his head at the sweet old woman. Mrs. Halloran's endless parade of stories had definitely lightened his mood. He hadn't realized how long they'd talked until he glanced at the clock. "Shit." He picked up the phone again and called Jensen's cell.

When the call went to Jensen's voice mail, a feeling of dread crept into Brian's heart. He quickly dug out the paper with Fisher's number and tried that, with no luck. *Shit.* After the conversation with Fisher earlier, he wondered if he could trust Marx to be alone with Jensen. Was he just being incredibly jealous or was there really something to worry about? He'd never been in love before. How was he supposed to know what men in love did or didn't do with ex-lovers? Brian cursed his battered body. He'd be more than happy to give Jensen sexual relief if that's what he needed.

He thought about the previous night. It was obvious Jensen had wanted more than a quick hand job. *Fuck!* Why hadn't he just sucked up the pain and let Jensen make love to him? He didn't need to worry about the Mundji killing any real chance he had at a relationship with Jensen. Brian seemed to be doing a fine job of that all by himself.

Thoughts of the Mundji swung his worries in a completely different direction. *What if something's happened to them? Shit!* While he'd been sitting there feeling sorry for himself, what if the Mundji had decided to exact its own brand of playtime on the man he loved?

Brian sprang from his chair and nearly doubled over in pain from pulling sutures. "Motherfucker," he ground out between clenched teeth, and steadied himself on the edge of the table. Once the nausea passed, Brian carefully turned, picked up a large knife from the counter, and walked slowly out the front door.

He'd never forgive himself if the Mundji had attacked Jensen and Fisher. He shrugged off the negativism. If they hadn't answered it wasn't because of misplaced feelings; it was because they *couldn't* answer. Brian had no doubt that whatever had happened to one had happened to both. Otherwise he would've heard something.

The outside prison door was propped open with a large rock. Brian sighed in relief. He hadn't even thought about how he would get in. Thankfully Jensen had done the thinking for him.

He made his way down the hall, looking through the various cells. Why hadn't he asked which section of the prison Jensen and Fisher would be working in? When he didn't immediately spot them, he slowly made his way up the stairs to the guards' catwalk. "Jensen!" he called, looking down on the individual cells. He started to panic when he didn't receive an answer.

With no visual on the two men, Brian went to the security console. Images flipped from room to room every couple of seconds. Brian held his breath, waiting for some sign of Jensen and Fisher's location. When the camera switched to a view of the library, Brian's heart stopped.

No. Oh God, no. With tears in his eyes, he made his way down the stairs to the library. Standing outside the room, he took a deep breath. Brian threw the door open and stared at the nightmare in front of him.

Jensen was naked, sitting on the edge of a library table with his legs wrapped around Fisher. The two men had been locked in a passionate kiss when he'd walked in, but quickly sprang apart. "Brian!" Jensen shouted. He jumped off the table and began picking his clothes up from the floor. "Brian, I can explain."

An equally nude Fisher chuckled. "Give it up, Jensen. He's never gonna believe my dick happened to find its way into your ass."

Brian covered his mouth and left the room. He stumbled down the corridor until he came to the cell Jensen and Fisher had been working on, before…

He lost the battle and vomited, spewing his breakfast into the clear acrylic toilet. He clenched his eyes shut as he heard bare running feet slap their way down the hall. He hated himself for believing the fairy tale he'd spun around his relationship with Jensen. *You're a fool, Brian Phipps.*

"Brian!" Jensen yelled, coming into the cell.

"Get out!" Brian screamed. He picked up the knife that had fallen beside the toilet and looked at the blade as it glinted in the overhead lights.

"Put the knife down," Jensen begged, his voice breaking.

Brian looked into Jensen's betraying eyes. "Get out and let me finish this." Brian crawled toward the single acrylic bed that Jensen and Fisher had separated from its top and filled with water.

Still gripping the knife, Brian raised his hands over the tub of water and slowed his breathing. Once he was centered, he began his prayer. "In the name of the Father, and the Son, and the Holy Spirit, amen." He said the prayer several times before turning the knife on himself.

"Brian!" Jensen lunged forward, trying to get the knife out of Brian's hand.

Brian's heated gaze flashed to Fisher. "You wanted him? You get him the hell out of here and let me do what I need to do."

Fisher rushed into the room and wrapped his muscular arms around Jensen's waist. "Let the man do what we're here for." Fisher grunted as he tried to muscle Jensen out of the cell.

"No!" Jensen screamed. "Not like this. I can't let him do this not knowing the—"

An *ooof* sounded as Fisher punched Jensen in the stomach.

Brian returned his attention to the task at hand. Instead of reopening one of the wounds on his back, Brian made a long slit across his forearm and plunged the bleeding cut into the blessed water. As he watched the water slowly turn pink, all he could think about was seeing Fisher and Jensen, their bodies nude and locked together in a passionate kiss.

He cursed as he felt the sob rising in his throat. "Dammit!" he screamed, tears dripping freely into the bloody water.

Brian's attention swung to the commotion in the corridor. Fisher Marx stood in front of the cell door as Jensen attempted to get around him. Brian's gaze was riveted to the muscles on display as the two strong men continued to grapple. The vision the two muscular men made was stunning, so incredible in fact, it almost pulled Brian's attention away from the vanquishing. He gripped the knife tighter, imagining the men in the throes of passion instead of wrestling outside the door.

He shook his head, coming back to the present. "Keep him out!" Brian shouted again. He was grateful that even as big as Jensen was, he was still no match for Fisher.

"I can't do this!" Jensen yelled. "Brian what you saw… it wasn't…"

Brian jumped as Fisher tackled Jensen and covered his mouth with both hands. "Shut the fuck up," Fisher growled, more menacing than Brian had ever heard him.

Brian realized something was seriously wrong. Given the tense situation, fighting may be natural, but there was definitely nothing natural about the way the two men were going at it. Brian looked around, opening himself. He could feel the Mundji's presence. *It's close.*

Bracing himself on the side of the acrylic bed, Brian stood and walked toward the cell wall. His eyes narrowed as he watched Fisher. Jensen's elbow shot out and clipped Fisher in the jaw. Fisher's head snapped back and Jensen used the advantage to shove the bigger man from his chest.

Left to their own devices, Brian had no doubt the men would kill each other. Brian opened the cell door. The air in the corridor snapped with electricity as the two men on the floor continued to wrestle for dominance. "Uh…guys?"

Jensen managed to straddle Fisher's chest. Brian was shocked when his lover wrapped his hands around Fisher's neck, pushing against his friend's windpipe. "Guys!" Brian shouted.

"I fucking hate this!" Jensen growled. Jensen looked over his shoulder. "I didn't want to do it, Birdie said…"

Brian was thrust forward onto the floor as the Mundji rushed to possess Jensen. "No!" Brian screamed, lunging toward the man he loved. Although his already-weakened body was no match for a man of Jensen's size, Brian threw himself in an attempt to knock the bigger man off balance. "Take me," he cried.

The momentary shift of Jensen's body was all Fisher needed to buck up and shove Jensen off of him. He scrambled backward and jumped into a crouched fighting stance. "What the hell's happening?"

"It's in him," Brian explained, trying to push Jensen into the cell. He could tell by Jensen's sluggish movements he was fighting the possession with everything he had. If they had a chance of getting his lover out of this alive, it was now. "Help me!"

Fisher wrapped his arms around Jensen's waist and helped Brian push him toward the cell. They were at the threshold when Jensen reached out and braced his hands against the cell walls, blocking any further attempt to shove him in the small cubicle.

Brian could tell the second the Mundji completely took over. Jensen looked over his shoulder and laughed, his breath so rank, nausea assailed Brian.

"Fuck," Fisher spat, trying to breathe through his mouth as Brian gagged and heaved where he stood.

Laughing maniacally, Jensen spun around and knocked Fisher and Brian to the floor. Brian stared wide-eyed as Jensen looked down at him. "I'm hungry," Jensen growled, rubbing his stomach. "You look like a nice little snack."

Jensen opened his mouth and a long, inhuman tongue slithered out to lick not only his lips, but his entire face, before flicking through the air toward Brian.

Brian scrambled backward, the forked tip of the Mundji's tongue going for his throat. Is this what happened to his granddad? Had the Mundji sucked him dry with that nasty pronged tongue?

Brian heard the electrical saw spur to life beside him. He didn't dare take his eyes off Jensen, but he hoped to hell Fisher hurried. "Don't kill him," Brian reminded Fisher. "Jensen's still in there somewhere."

The saw screamed in Brian's ear as Fisher charged toward the four-foot-long tongue. A split second before the spinning blade connected, Jensen turned his head and waved his hand, sending Fisher flying through the air.

Brian watched in horror as Fisher's body connected with one of the acrylic walls. The force was so strong, the thick plastic cracked on impact. "No!" Brian screamed, as Fisher's lifeless body slid to the floor, leaving a trail of blood in its wake.

Knowing he was on his own to save the man he loved, Brian lurched forward, scrambling through Jensen's legs and into the cell. Lunging for the discarded knife, Brian was suddenly pulled backward. Knife in his grip, Brian rolled over just as twin points of pain dug into his sutured calf.

Swinging the knife wildly, Brian managed to cut off the tip of the Mundji's unholy tongue. The Mundji's loud shriek had Brian involuntarily dropping the knife and covering his ears.

Get him in the water. Brian lowered his hand and picked the weapon up once more. He dived toward the bed filled with water and faced the Mundji. "You can't touch me in here, you evil sonofabitch!"

He took a deep breath, and prepared for the attack he knew was coming. Before his eyes, the Mundji's tongue regenerated, forming two more deadly prongs. The evil laugh emanating from Jensen sent shivers through Brian's weak and bleeding body.

The regeneration was something Brian hadn't counted on. He knew the Mundji could play cat and mouse with him all day. He quickly tried to devise another avenue of attack. If his plan had any hope of working, he'd need both hands. Brian dropped the knife to the bottom of the makeshift bathtub and summoned all the strength he had left.

When the Mundji's tongue was within reach, Brian stretched out and wrapped his hands around the slithering, slimy appendage above the prongs. He jerked back toward himself with everything he had and was rewarded when Jensen's body was thrown off balance, tumbling into the pool on top of him.

The bloody holy water had no effect on the Mundji except to make it furious. *Because I'm no longer his last victim, it has to be Jensen's blood.* Jensen's hands wrapped around Brian's neck and pushed him under the water, the creature's deadly tongue latching onto Brian's neck.

Brian felt the life force slowly being drained from his body and searched the bottom of the tub for the dropped weapon. He felt the slick surface of the blade and grabbed it, slicing his own hand in the process. His lungs began to burn with the lack of oxygen as he struggled with the knife. By the time Brian worked the handle into his grip, he barely had the strength to lift it. Plunging the blade into the thigh of the man he loved was the hardest thing he'd ever had to do. Brian prayed he hadn't hit a major artery.

As blood began flowing from the open wound, the Mundji's tongue pulled from Brian's neck. He knew he had no more than ten seconds of air left in his lungs. Sending up a quick prayer, Brian squeezed Jensen's punctured thigh, sending more of his precious blood into the water.

He suddenly felt soothing warmth invade him as he continued to struggle in the bloody water. Without knowing how, he felt like Jensen was becoming a part of him. Brian welcomed the warmth with open arms. If this was the last thing he'd ever share with the man he loved, he wanted to embrace it. The episode with Fisher earlier still hurt, but in the grip of death, Brian didn't want to go to his grave with anything but love in his heart.

Jensen's body lurched, thrashing wildly, bringing Brian back to the battle at hand. Given the opportunity, he pushed the heavy body off his chest and resurfaced, gulping for much-needed oxygen. After reversing positions, Brian submerged Jensen's body as he continued to draw air into his long-deprived lungs. "Come on. Come on," he prayed, as he counted silently.

With one last desperate attempt at survival, the Mundji plunged the forgotten knife in Brian's side. Brian screamed in pain and brought his elbow down on Jensen's face as the water turned an even darker shade of crimson.

Jensen's body jerked once more before going limp. Brian waited ten more seconds before lifting his lover's head out of the water. "Live, dammit," he cried as his own breathing became more labored.

Brian knew it was imperative to get them both out of the altered acrylic bed before he passed out. He didn't know where he found the strength, but he eventually pushed Jensen's upper body over the edge. Brian climbed out and landed on the floor, his hand automatically going to his side. He knew the knife had punctured his lung, but saving Jensen was the most important thing to him at that moment. Brian looked toward the doorway.

Crossing the distance needed to reach Fisher's cell phone seemed unattainable. Each movement proved laborious, as his now-opened wounds continued to bleed, covering him in a crimson suit of agony. Brian concentrated on putting one arm in front of the other as he dragged himself across the floor, leaving a vibrant red trail in his wake.

He had no idea how long it took him to reach Fisher's limp and bleeding body, but Brian managed to unclip the phone from the man's belt. He turned it on and looked at the display screen. He knew if he called the WPU they were as good as dead, so he managed to punch in 9-1-1.

"Nine-one-one operator. What is the nature of your emergency?" the welcomed voice said.

Brian was panting and wheezing. It took three tries before he could whisper. "Three critically wounded at Alcatraz." Brian wheezed again. "In the prison. We're the only ones here." He passed out before the operator could reply.

CHAPTER TEN

An argument woke Brian. He opened his eyes and stared at the acoustic tiled ceiling, trying to get his bearings.

"It's not your fault!" Fisher hissed.

"The hell it's not. I should never have done what that crazy bitch told me to do. Now I may never get the chance to tell him the truth."

Confused by Jensen's words, Brian tried to talk. It was then that he realized he had a tube down his throat. He grunted to get his lover's attention.

"Brian?" Jensen's face appeared, looming over him. "Oh my God." Jensen looked to his left. "Get a doctor," he ordered.

Brian heard footsteps running out of the room. Jensen turned his attention back to Brian. "Oh, baby, I thought I'd lost you forever," Jensen said, peppering Brian's face with kisses.

Brian tried to shake his head no, but passed out before he completed the action.

* * * *

Jensen's throat hurt like hell after almost three weeks spent reading anything and everything to the man he loved. The doctors tried to assure him Brian's coma was necessary for his body's recovery, but Jensen refused to believe it. He longed to once again see those deep green eyes he'd fallen in love with. It had been nearly a week since Brian had woken briefly. In all, Jensen had spent nineteen and a half days praying his lover would recover.

It turned out that Jensen had been the lucky one among the three. The wound on his thigh had been relatively easy for the doctors to sew. He'd been released two days later and had spent the next four days alternating between Brian and Fisher's bedsides.

Fisher had suffered a severe concussion, requiring a drainage tube to keep the fluid from building up in his skull. Once he was assured Fisher would make a full recovery, Jensen had attached himself to Brian's side and could rarely be convinced to leave, even to smoke.

Something he hadn't mentioned to either the doctors or Fisher was the feeling that part of him was missing. Jensen didn't know if he could even explain it to them if he tried. He'd chalked it up to his remorse over what had happened to Brian, but something at the back of his mind told him it was more than that.

"How is he?" Fisher's deep voice interrupted Jensen's thoughts.

"The same," he answered. The guilt he felt over the episode in the library still ate at him. How could he have let Brian think he'd had sex with Fisher? Just remembering the hurt in Brian's eyes when he'd walked into the library brought tears to Jensen's eyes. He didn't know if he'd ever get a chance to make things right and it was eating him alive.

"Hey," Fisher said, coming to stand behind Jensen. A strong hand squeezed his shoulder as Fisher showed his quiet support.

"I've tried every day to explain to him why we had to deceive him, but he's still given no sign he's heard me." Jensen lifted Brian's hand and kissed it. He looked over his shoulder at his friend. "Where've you been?"

"On the phone trying to get both our butts out of the sling."

"Did you tell them what Brian said about going to the press?" Jensen asked.

"Yeah. The WPU's finally agreed to bury the bones from the lighthouse and drop the charges against me."

"So what's the problem?" As far as Jensen knew, that was everything they'd asked for in exchange for their silence.

"I'm trying to get our pensions. I've become somewhat accustomed to a certain kind of lifestyle, one I can't maintain on a cop's salary." Fisher chuckled.

"Greedy bastard," Jensen teased.

"Yep."

A twitch from one of Brian's fingers had Jensen rising to his feet. "Brian?" He bent over his lover. "Do it again, baby. Come on. Open those pretty eyes for me."

He watched as Brian's lashes fluttered against his cheeks for several seconds before going dormant again. "Fuck!" Jensen cursed.

* * * *

Brian opened his eyes and smiled. Fisher was sound asleep in the chair next to his bed, snoring up a storm. "Hey," he rasped, trying to get the big man to wake up. His voice barely audible, Brian knew he'd never be heard over Fisher's snore. He blindly reached for the call button on the rail of his bed.

A nurse's voice sounded over the speaker. "Yes?"

"Water." Brian wasn't sure if the nurse heard him or not, but several seconds later a young woman came bustling into the room.

"Well, Sleeping Beauty is finally awake." She grinned, spooning two ice chips into Brian's mouth.

Brian let the ice melt on his tongue. He knew for a fact he'd never tasted anything so sweet. When the last of the water had trickled its way down his parched throat, he opened for more, feeling like a baby bird.

"One more." The nurse responded to his gesture.

Brian gestured toward the still sleeping Fisher with a question in his eyes. The nurse grinned. "The other one is out in the lobby asleep on the sofa. They've been taking turns for the past several weeks."

Brian swallowed the water. "How long?"

The nurse adjusted the blankets around Brian with a sympathetic expression. "You were brought in almost four weeks ago."

Four weeks? "Jensen?"

"He's fine. I'll go wake him for you. You'll have to be quiet though. It's way after visiting hours, but none of us have had the heart to run your two men out of here."

The nurse's words sank in and Brian shook his head. "Only one man. Jensen."

She grinned and patted his hand. "If you say so."

Confused, Brian watched her walk out. He wondered what had happened since he'd been out. The scene in the library flashed through his mind. Were Fisher and Jensen a couple? Had he lost his man forever?

Jensen came into the room. "Oh God, I'm so happy to see you awake." Jensen placed a soft kiss on Brian's lips.

Brian looked into Jensen's tear-filled eyes. He wanted to ask so many questions but his voice wouldn't cooperate.

Jensen must've seen the confusion in Brian's expression. "You're gonna be okay, baby." Jensen smoothed Brian's hair away from his forehead. "You need to get some more rest, but I need to tell you something first."

Brian braced himself for Jensen's blow-off.

"I need you to know I didn't have sex with Fisher. It was a setup, one that I've kicked myself for ever since. Birdie Cox told us in order for you to be successful in vanquishing the Mundji, you needed hate in your heart. She said it was up to me to do whatever was necessary to make you hate me." Jensen stopped talking and dried his eyes on his shirtsleeve.

"I had no idea how bad it would really be. If I'd known, I never would've agreed to any of it. Birdie made it sound like your life depended on it. She said that if we didn't take care of the Mundji it would continue to follow you forever. I knew you didn't want that. I was just trying to do the right thing." Jensen leaned down, brushed a kiss across Brian's forehead.

"Did you hear me, babe? We set it up, all of it. Fisher telling you he still loved me. You finding us naked. All of it. I guess what I hadn't counted on was hating myself more for doing it than you did. That's why that thing came after me. It followed the biggest source of hatred."

They hadn't fucked? A blanket of peace seemed to cover Brian at that moment. His eyes drifted shut, secure in the fact he'd live to love Jensen forever.

* * * *

"Wakey, wakey," Jensen cooed, kissing Brian.

Brian opened his mouth, sucking Jensen's tongue inside. The kisses they'd shared in the last several days had been the best of their relationship, and Brian couldn't seem to get enough.

Jensen chuckled and pulled back. Brian opened his eyes to the gorgeous face of his lover. "They're letting you out," Jensen declared. "The doctor even said he thought it would be okay for us to fly to Colorado at the end of the week."

Going back home felt like a dream, but he still continued to have nightmares about Alcatraz. "You really think we got them all?" He didn't have to explain further; Jensen knew exactly what he was asking. Since waking up from the coma, the two of them seemed to read each other's minds quite effectively. He had an idea of why, but the two of them had yet to talk about it.

"Seems so. They've already moved the inmates back into the prison. I spoke with Phil earlier in the week. The WPU made him acting warden."

"Does it seem weird to you? I mean after all these years you're suddenly without a job?" Brian knew Jensen's work ethic wouldn't handle unemployment well.

"What? I thought you already offered me a job. What about the nice bookstore owner who enjoys blowing his favored employees in the back room? It's the only reason I agreed to such a drastic pay cut."

Brian couldn't keep from laughing. "And if you're an exceptional employee, I may offer several bonuses throughout the day."

"Now you're just teasing me." Jensen chuckled before swiping his tongue over Brian's lips.

Brian shook his head. "Employee relations are my number one priority from now on."

EPILOGUE

Ten months later

Mrs. Halloran picked up her purse and slung it over her shoulder. "I'll be back in one hour, not a moment longer." She eyed Jensen and Brian with a warning.

"Yes, ma'am," Jensen replied, tipping his head. They'd been caught three days earlier, his dick buried to the hilt in Brian's ass, when Mrs. Halloran returned from lunch early.

As soon as the older woman shut the front door, Brian locked it and put the "Out to Lunch" sign up. Turning back to Jensen, Brian leaned against the door. "I thought she'd never leave."

Jensen started unbuttoning his shirt as he turned and strolled toward the back of the shop. "Thank God for slow afternoons," he said, letting his shirt fall to the stockroom floor.

He heard Brian close the door, seconds before his lover's shirt flew through the air. "Ooh, someone's in a hurry."

"You've been teasing me all day," Brian said, running his hands up Jensen's chest.

Before he had a chance to get his jeans off, Brian had already attached his lips to Jensen's nipple. Jensen moaned. He wasn't sure which he loved more, the feel of the smaller man's tongue and teeth playing with his nipple, or how horny Brian became while doing it.

Jensen insinuated his hands between their bodies and pushed down his jeans and underwear before going to work on Brian's clothes. As soon as he had Brian's pants pushed down, Jensen wiggled his hips, painting his lover's belly with his pre-cum. "Feel that? You're killing me, babe," Jensen groaned.

He slowly walked backward until the backs of his knees came into contact with the old couch they'd brought in. At first Mrs. Halloran hadn't understood why they needed a couch in the stockroom when they already had several strewn through the store, but after catching them in the act, she hadn't mentioned it again.

Jensen sat down and pulled a blissfully naked Brian into his lap. It had been ten months since they'd set up house together, and Jensen was grateful for every single day. For the first time in his life, he was living instead of simply existing. "It's your turn to choose. Top or bottom?" Jensen asked, sliding his fingers down the crack of Brian's ass.

"I think you've already made the choice." Brian chuckled, reaching for the lube hidden under the sofa cushion.

Jensen grinned. He loved getting his way, especially when his way was deep into Brian's hot hole. He held out his hand and Brian dribbled a good amount of slick onto it. "Are you complaining?" he asked. Jensen rimmed Brian's hole for a few seconds before delving inside.

"Are you nuts?" Brian lifted off Jensen's lap and rode the two fingers easing their way in his ass.

Jensen's other hand smoothed down Brian's back, feeling the mapwork of scars. Some might find it odd, but Jensen touched the scars on a daily basis. They served to remind him how lucky he was that they'd both survived the ghosts of Alcatraz.

"I'm ready," Brian moaned.

Pushing the disturbing thoughts of their ordeal aside for the moment, Jensen used the extra lube on his hand to grease his cock. He grabbed the back of Brian's head and pulled his lover in for a deep kiss as he buried himself balls-deep in the place he called home.

Their fucking was brutal, as it so often was. Jensen blamed it on the never-ending passion the two had for each other, but Brian blamed it on something else entirely. According to Brian, when they'd bathed in the tub of holy water, their blood had combined, creating a bond that would never be sated, never be broken.

As Brian continued to ride him, Jensen began to think Brian might be right. Their love transcended anything he'd ever known. Jensen sensed Brian's mood before his love even entered the room. Several months ago, Brian had cut himself chopping vegetables, and Jensen had known immediately he needed to get home.

Jensen leaned forward, rolling them both to the cold tile floor. "Deeper," he grunted, slipping Brian's legs over his shoulders. He held Brian's ass off the ground as his hips pistoned at lightning speed, burying himself to the hilt with every thrust.

He looked down into the green depths of Brian's eyes. "I love you."

Jacking his cock, Brian gave Jensen a heavy-lidded stare. "I know. I feel it." Brian's body jerked under Jensen's as a long string of pearls shot their way from the head of Brian's cock.

Jensen felt the heat splatter onto his chest, and answered the call by filling Brian's body with his seed. His body bucked as the climax continued to rack his body.

After being milked dry, Jensen collapsed to the side of his lover. They lay wrapped around each other for several blissful moments before Jensen's phone started to buzz.

"Dammit," he mumbled, looking across the floor at his jeans. He rolled over and stretched out his arm, managing to snag the leg of his pants. He pulled the jeans toward him and dug the phone out of his pocket.

"Black," he answered, snuggling back up to Brian.

"It's too early in the day for you to be that tired, unless you've been fucking." Fisher laughed.

Jensen was too sated and happy to rise to Fisher's bait. "What do you want?"

"Just to ask your opinion on something."

"Okay, shoot." He felt Brian's lips working their way down his neck to his nipples.

"Well, I was at this county law enforcement picnic thing last night, and I overheard something that's been bugging me ever since."

Jensen couldn't keep a bark of laughter from erupting. "Somehow I just can't picture you playing nice at a picnic."

"Shut the hell up, this isn't about me trying to fit in with the locals, it's about a kid who's being hurt," Fisher growled, his normally deep voice dropping even lower.

That got Jensen's attention immediately. Brian must've felt the tension creep into Jensen's body, because his lover released his nipple and sat up. "What's going on?" Brian asked.

Jensen covered the mouthpiece. "I don't know yet. Hold on."

"What's happening to the kid?" Jensen asked Fisher.

"Well, the guys were making jokes about how this weird kid had a long history of making false police reports about his dad hurting him. The kid even went to the emergency room a couple of times saying he'd been raped."

"Have they questioned the father?" Jensen asked.

"Well, see, that's the strange part; the kid's dad's been dead for over six years."

The hair on the back of Jensen's neck stood up. "You think it could be a ghost?"

"That's why I'm calling. I thought I'd get your and Brian's take on it. I haven't met the kid yet, but according to the guys, he's only twenty-two. He's been on his own since his mom ran off a year after his dad died, claiming the boy was too violent to live with."

Jensen gripped the phone tighter. He hated the thought of getting involved with another pissed-off ghost. "I'll put Brian on the phone." He started to give the phone to his lover, but stopped and put it back to his ear. "Fisher?"

"Yeah."

"No matter what happens, be careful. I almost lost you once—"

"I will," Fisher said, cutting him off. "I just can't sit back and do nothing. From the sounds of it, the boy's pretty much become a hermit. He's too damn young to give up on life like that."

Jensen smiled. Fisher's heart always was as big as his body. "Okay. Here's Brian." Jensen handed the phone off and got to his feet. He hated the thought of Fisher taking on something like they'd dealt with in California alone, but he also couldn't take the chance of putting Brian into harm's way again.

"Okay, call us if you need us," Brian said and snapped the phone shut.

"Well?" Jensen asked, handing Brian his clothes.

Brian shimmied into his underwear and pants before he spoke. "Sounds like another level two, since it's actually hurting the boy."

"Fisher isn't gonna try and take it on, is he?"

"Hmmm, good question. I told him to try and get the kid away from the house. If he's lucky, the spirit will be tied to the dwelling, not the boy."

"And if it's not?"

"Then I told him to call us," Brian said in a matter-of-fact tone.

Jensen swung Brian into his arms and kissed him. "I thought we agreed no more ghost chasing."

Brian ran his fingers through the short patch of hair on Jensen's chest. "We did. I'm not chasing though, I'm helping a friend. There's a difference."

Jensen groaned and nipped Brian's shoulder. He knew his partner was right, but that didn't mean he had to like it. "Life with you is never going to be boring, is it?"

Brian pulled Jensen's head down for another passionate kiss. "Not if I can help it.

THE END

THE CLAIMING OF
PATRICK
DONNELLY

CAROL LYNNE

CHAPTER ONE

Fisher Marx woke with a start. He sat straight up and used the tangled sheet to wipe the sweat from his face and head. "Christ."

He swung his legs over the side of the mattress and stumbled to the bathroom. After emptying his bladder, Fisher ran some cold water in the sink and splashed his face. The dream he'd had since making it out of Alcatraz alive had morphed into a whole new nightmare, thanks to the Hickory County policemen's picnic he'd attended hours earlier.

His thoughts kept returning to the story he'd overheard about the boy, Patrick Donnelly. How the group of men could joke about anyone being abused was beyond him. It had been hard enough getting the group of good ol' boys to allow an African American into their tight little clique. The fact that his old Marine buddy, Conner Diggs had pretty much created a spot for him, hadn't helped matters either, and now this. He began to wonder whether he'd ever fit into the small town mindset.

Fisher didn't give a damn that the cops thought the kid's story was nothing more than an overactive imagination, and he'd told them that in no uncertain terms. He'd seen some seriously fucked up shit on Alcatraz Island. No longer was he the type of man who scoffed at the supernatural.

He turned off the tap and dried his face on a hand towel, before going to the kitchen for a drink. He poured a finger of light mahogany liquid into a highball glass and held it up. In his opinion, one of the best things about eighteen-year-old single malt was its nose. He inhaled the fragrances of dried fruit, ginger, citrus, and vanilla, before taking his first sip.

With drink in hand, Fisher walked to the living room and sank into the couch. He glanced at the clock on the DVD player and groaned. There was no way he'd be able to keep himself from falling asleep. At barely three in the morning, Fisher knew he'd once again need to face his demons before the night was through.

He took another sip of his whiskey and got up to retrieve his laptop from his desk. After powering it up, he typed in the url for the Hickory County newspaper, and then more specifically, the name James Donnelly.

Several articles came up on Patrick Donnelly's father. The first was from a police report listing, citing a call to the residence for a domestic disturbance. The second was a much bigger article on the suicide of James Donnelly, along with an old picture of him. The photograph was of Donnelly in his Navy dress uniform.

Fisher read the article thoroughly. It seemed James stuck the end of a shotgun into his mouth in front of his only child, Patrick. *Fuck.*

Fisher took another sip, before rubbing the smooth glass over his forehead and selecting the url for the next article. He bit his lip as a picture of James Donnelly loaded onto the screen. The headline read, *Local Teacher Assaulted.*

He leaned closer to the screen. There was something about the photo of the man that didn't seem right, but he couldn't put his finger on it. The article included a detailed account from another teacher at Toblerville High School. According to the story, James was found beaten and bleeding in his classroom on a Monday morning. By all accounts, James had suffered ongoing abuse since the Friday before. No suspects had ever been found or charged in the assault, but James resigned his teaching position shortly after being released from the hospital.

Fisher bookmarked the page in case he needed it later. The back of his neck began to prickle at the similarities between the stories he'd heard about Patrick Donnelly and the one he'd just read about James. He scratched the bristles of his goatee and closed the laptop.

He finished off his whiskey and leaned back on the sofa. The next logical step was to research Patrick, but Fisher knew he'd never get to sleep if he started reading about the kid. He turned and stretched out on the couch, his large hands resting on his stomach.

In the moments before sleep overtook him, Fisher decided he would put a call in to Jensen and Brian later that morning. He knew Jensen's stand on Brian messing with the paranormal again, but Fisher had a feeling he'd need all the advice Brian could give him.

* * * *

Patrick Donnelly studied the pile of black curls on the kitchen floor. He set the hair trimmer on the table and ran his hands over his freshly shorn head, being careful to avoid the raw patch of skin. He'd be damned if his father would be able to pull him across the room by his hair again.

He could tell by the feel of it, he'd done a piss-poor job, but he didn't dare look in a mirror to cut it. The hair at his feet began to swirl, rising up like a black tornado.

He spat into the eye of the storm with satisfaction. "Take that, you sonofabitch."

Patrick knew what was coming, even before it started. He braced himself against the kitchen table as unseen hands raked across his flesh. He swallowed the rising bile as his cock was enveloped in a mysterious warmth. *Shit*. Had he turned the dirty fucker on instead of repulsing him with his new appearance?

The pain he could handle, but he'd be damned if he'd allow himself to be sexually used again, without a fight. He spun around and fled the room, knocking the invisible hands and mouth from his body.

A blow to the side of his head knocked Patrick to the living room floor. Instinctively, he curled into a fetal position with his back against the sofa. Another set of raw scratches appeared on his side as his father's hands neared his ass. After six years, he didn't know why he continued to fight the inevitable.

* * * *

Keys in hand, Fisher locked the front door before climbing behind the wheel of his pickup. After his phone conversation with Jensen and Brian, he'd been galvanized to do something for the kid as soon as possible, but he'd had to work his normal shift. Now that he was off the clock and had changed out of his uniform, he was ready to face whatever horror Patrick was dealing with.

Brian, a friend and damn good ex-parapsychologist, had agreed with him that Patrick's troubles sounded spirit related. Fisher hoped he'd be able to convince the young man to leave the house with him. He still wasn't sure what he'd do with Patrick once they were safely away, but first he'd need to convince the boy he believed him.

Fisher consulted the directions he'd obtained from the internet and turned onto a seldom-used dirt driveway at a rather steep incline. Despite the high undercarriage of his truck, Fisher heard the bottom scrape on the rutted dirt path on several occasions, wincing each time. How long had it been since the driveway had been graded?

The Donnelly residence appeared once he rounded the last bend. Gooseflesh immediately covered his skin as he studied the rundown house. Typical of older homes, the front porch sagged, giving the house the appearance of sliding forward into the yard. If the house had once been painted, there was no longer evidence of the deed. The overall structure looked abandoned, not something a young man would live in.

He parked on a sparsely covered patch of lawn he assumed used to be the driveway and got out to stand beside his truck. He'd decided against wearing his uniform, opting for blue jeans and a faded gray Philadelphia Eagles T-shirt instead.

Fisher walked toward the front porch, running the tips of his fingers over his goatee. The addition of the beard to match up with his moustache was fairly new, and he still wasn't used to the texture against his skin.

He kept watch for weak boards as he climbed the steps onto the aging porch. With a deep breath, he knocked on the frame of the ripped screen door and waited. Fear wasn't a word in Fisher's vocabulary until he'd gone up against the ghosts of Alcatraz, but he'd been shown firsthand the things that could go bump in the night.

When he received no answer, Fisher knocked again more forcefully. After several moments, the yellowed eyelet curtain covering the door's window moved to the side. Fisher could barely make out a face from the dark interior.

"Patrick? My name's Fisher Marx. Could I talk to you for a minute?"

The hand holding the curtain retreated and Fisher was once again cut-off. He waited, hoping he'd hear the click of a lock releasing.

When nothing happened, he spoke through the door again. "I heard what's been happening to you, and I think I can help."

Still nothing. Fisher was contemplating breaking the door down, when it suddenly opened a crack.

"You can't help me," a soft voice replied.

Although Fisher couldn't see the boy's face, the raw-knuckled hand holding the edge of the door was enough to shore up his resolve to help. He decided honesty would be the best course of action.

"Ten months ago, two of my friends and I took on a prison full of ghosts. They damn near killed us, but we managed to survive. You can trust me when I tell ya I believe you."

"How'd you do it?" Patrick asked from behind the door.

"My friend Brian is an expert in parapsychology. He knew how to vanquish the level twos, but it took a leap of faith to send the Mundji back to hell."

"Level two? Mundji?"

Fisher sighed and wiped the sweat from the top of his shaven head. "Can I get you to open the door so we can talk about this face to face?"

After several heartbeats, the door started to open. Fisher got his first look at Patrick's bruised and swollen face a split second before the door slammed shut. He heard Patrick cry out and went into action.

"Get away from the door!" Fisher screamed as he kicked the door with everything he had.

The door splintered enough, after several well-placed kicks, to open. Fisher shouldered his way into the house and stopped in his tracks as Patrick sailed through the air in front of him.

He rushed toward the young man as Patrick's body slammed into the wall with a sickening thud. Without thought, Fisher scooped an unconscious Patrick into his arms and raced for the door. He was two steps away from the threshold when the entire house began to shake as an enraged scream filled the interior. With no time or desire to see what it was, Fisher skirted the broken door and made it out of the house.

Once on the porch, Fisher continued on to his truck. He doubted he'd ever moved so fast in his life. He managed to get Patrick into the cab, before climbing in after him. He started the engine and threw the pickup in gear as Patrick started to come around.

While trying to avoid some of the ruts in the drive, Fisher reached down and checked the back of Patrick's head for blood. When all he felt was a large bump, he breathed a sigh of relief.

Once he made it to the county road, he pulled the truck to the shoulder and parked. For the first time, Fisher got a good look at Patrick. His hand drifted over the man's scalp, feeling healed lacerations and the soft stubble of black half-inch hair.

The longer he studied the road map of scars, the angrier he became. How could any doctor examine this man and not see the clear signs of abuse?

He felt a tightening in his chest at the thought of Patrick suffering alone for so many years. He tried to imagine facing the ghosts back at Alcatraz alone. Fisher closed his eyes and shook his head. He knew without a doubt that he wouldn't have survived. So, how had a skinny, scared twenty-two year old managed it for so long? It took everything in him not to pull the young man into his arms to shield him from the hurtful world he'd come to know.

Patrick's long black lashes began to flutter a moment before they opened to reveal troubled dark blue eyes. Patrick seemed quite surprised to see Fisher hovering over him. He held the back of his head as he tried to sit up.

"You need to get me back to the house."

Fisher shook his head. "I need to get you to a hospital. More than likely you've got a nasty concussion."

Patrick shook his head. "I've had them before. I don't need a doctor to tell me what to do for one."

Before Fisher could say anything further, Patrick scooted over to the passenger's door and opened it. Stunned by the sudden movement, it took Fisher several seconds to get out of the truck and reach the young man who'd already started back up his drive.

"What're you doing? You can't go back there," he said as he moved to stand in front of Patrick.

Patrick looked up at Fisher. "It'll only get worse if I don't. He'll eventually find me."

That answered Fisher's earlier question. "So the spirit is attached to you and not the house?"

Patrick nodded and tried to step around Fisher. "I'm sorry. I know you're trying to help, but I'm beginning to think the only thing that'll stop it, is doing just what dad did, and blow my own head off."

Too much information was hurtling toward him. Fisher needed a moment to process and figure out his next step. "How long before it finds you again?"

Patrick shrugged. "It's different each time. Sometimes hours, sometimes a few days. But the longer it takes, the worse it is when he finds me."

Fisher had to lean forward in order to hear the younger man's soft voice. He wondered if the timid, almost shy way of speaking was caused by years of abuse, or the isolation he'd been forced to endure. He knew leaving Patrick to go back to the hell he'd just escaped wasn't an option.

"Come home with me. I need to make a phone call, and I can't leave you here."

Patrick shook his head. "I don't know why you wanna help me, but it's no use. I've read everything I could get my hands on. There's nothing."

Fisher couldn't explain why he felt the overwhelming desire to help, other than it wasn't in his character to watch someone suffer. Even though defeat was clearly stamped on Patrick's bruised face, his eyes held a tiny sparkle of hope. Fisher clung to that gaze, getting lost in their blue depths.

Without knowing why, Fisher reached out and pulled Patrick into his arms. The small man's body went stiff as a board, but Fisher refused to let go. He knew he needed to figure out whether Patrick was afraid of being held, or simply unaccustomed to human touch.

"I'm not going to hurt you," Fisher whispered. "I only want to comfort you. To let you know you're not alone."

Patrick's body relaxed slightly, but he still didn't reciprocate the embrace. Fisher released his hold and stepped back. "Will you please let me take you away from here until I figure a few things out?"

Patrick's tongue snaked out to run over the healing cut on his lower lip. Fisher could see the indecision in the small man's eyes. "If you're worried about me, don't. I know what I'm getting into."

"It's not that. I think I'm the only one he hates. You're the first person to ever see what he's capable of." Patrick looked down toward his feet. "It's the reason no one's ever believed me."

"So that whole tossing you around thing is new?"

"No, but on the rare occasion that someone comes to the door, he's usually quiet. I don't think he wants people to know about him. The fact that he did that to me in front of you is a first," Patrick explained.

"Do *you* ever see him?" Fisher asked as he steered Patrick back to the pickup.

Patrick shook his head as he climbed in the passenger side. "I see him in mirrors, but it's not him. I mean, it's him, I know it is, but he uses a different face once in a while. I think it's so he can mess with my mind."

Fisher started the truck and pulled back onto the road toward town. He glanced at Patrick several times out of the corner of his eye. The younger man seemed to be chewing his thumbnail down to the quick.

He hated to question Patrick about the identity of his abuser, but he needed answers. "Are you sure it's your dad's ghost that's hurting you?"

Patrick squeezed his eyes shut. "I know what he feels like when he beats me and does the other stuff."

"Other stuff?" Fisher questioned.

"He rapes me when he's really mad," Patrick confessed.

Fisher sucked in a sharp breath. *Fuck.* He tapped his hand on the steering wheel until the sound of his ring clicking against the surface started bugging even him. *Get a grip.*

"How long has this been going on?" he finally asked.

Patrick's hand dropped to his lap. "You mean how long since my dad's been dead, or before that?"

Fisher's gut clenched. He should've realized when he read the newspaper articles that James Donnelly's bizarre behavior would've manifested at home, too. "Both, I guess."

"The first time he came into my room was my sixteenth birthday. He killed himself two months later," Patrick mumbled.

"And nothing before that?" Fisher had been around his fair share of criminals, and he knew most child molesters started much earlier.

Patrick shook his head. "I think maybe his dad did it to him. I remember him saying something like that one night."

That certainly fit the pattern. Patrick's index finger went into his mouth as he began chewing at the nail. Fisher was surprised the guy had any nails left to chew on. "You hungry? I could run through the drive-thru."

Patrick started to say something, then shook his head.

"You're not hungry?" Fisher prodded.

"I don't have any money," Patrick answered.

"With the way I rushed you out of the house, I didn't figure you would have. It's my treat."

When Patrick didn't immediately agree, Fisher continued. "Look, the truth is, I'm starving, and I'll feel like a real shit if I eat in front of you."

Patrick looked sideways at Fisher, as if he knew exactly what he was trying to do, but eventually nodded.

Toblerville didn't have much, but there was a McDonald's and a drive-thru mom–and-pop place on the way to his house. "Do you like Blevin's okay?"

Patrick shrugged. "Never ate there."

"Really? Would you prefer McDonald's?" Fisher asked.

Once again, Patrick shrugged. "Never ate there either. You choose."

"Blevin's it is." Trying to fill the time with small talk, Fisher continued. "So you usually cook your own meals?"

Patrick abandoned his finger to chew on the side of his lower lip that wasn't cut. "I usually just eat the vegetables and stuff from the garden, the electricity's been turned off for a while now."

Fisher studied Patrick for a few moments. What he'd taken as a lean build was evidently malnutrition. He wondered how the young man was even alive. He knew from listening to the gossip that Patrick didn't leave his house, which probably meant he didn't have the ability to earn money. How had he survived for so long without an income? Fisher knew he'd eventually get the details of Patrick's life, but he also knew pushing the younger man would only lead to trouble.

"Well, we'll get us a couple of burgers and sides and take them back to my place."

He couldn't help but wonder how long Patrick's electricity had been off. Had he suffered through the winter without it? It was one more thing to add to the list of injustices done to the younger man.

Fisher pulled up to the drive-thru window. Blevin's wasn't as fancy as McDonald's. You had to place your order face-to-face, instead of through an intercom. He leaned out the window and spoke to the attractive young lady, who not only looked bored but irritated that someone had bothered her.

"Give me three double cheeseburgers, two large fries, an onion ring and two of the biggest Cokes you have."

Little Miss Sunshine turned without saying a word and put their order in. Fisher doubted Emmett and Charlene Blevin would approve of the customer service currently being doled out. They were a sweet older couple who'd owned the hamburger stand for over thirty years.

Fisher noticed Patrick didn't even look the girl's way. "Do you know her?"

Patrick turned away from the passenger window, fingernail between his teeth, and nodded. "She went to my high school," he said around his finger.

"Well, I hope she's a nicer person than she is a waitress," Fisher commented.

Patrick shrugged. "Wouldn't know."

Fisher knew the graduates in Toblerville only numbered around fifty per class, so either Patrick was ignored, or had been treated badly by the girl. He found his gaze going back to the unfriendly waitress. He spotted her giggling with one of the guys behind the counter. Fisher heard the girl mention Patrick's name as she continued to laugh and point toward the truck before she saw him watching her.

An almost blind rage overtook Fisher. He leaned farther out of his truck window and shouted inside the small drive-thru window. "Keep your food, but you can bet I'll be speaking to the Blevins." Fisher put the pickup in gear and pulled away from the restaurant. "So, I guess McDonald's is on the menu."

Patrick removed the fingernail from his mouth and scratched at the short hair on top of his head. "Sorry."

"For what?"

Patrick gestured to the drive-thru they'd just left. "People are uncomfortable around me."

"I'm not," Fisher replied. He realized it was the truth. *Strange.* He was every bit of twenty-two years older than Patrick, so why did he already feel such a connection to him?

Out of the corner of his eye, he noticed Patrick studying him for several moments, before turning back to the window.

Fisher started to say more, but stopped himself. *Best to leave things alone for now.* He drove up to the golden arches and ordered. Within minutes, he was pulling away with two large sacks of food on the seat beside him.

"Hope you like Coke. Guess I should've asked." Fisher watched as Patrick unwrapped his straw and took a sip of his large beverage. The involuntary smile on Patrick's boyish face said it all.

"I haven't had a Coke in years. It's good."

The simple statement pretty much summed up Patrick's life in the years since his abuse began. How many people took something as simple as a fucking Coke for granted? Fisher didn't even want to think about it. He felt ashamed of himself for the extravagances he indulged in.

He pulled into his driveway and parked in front of the two-car garage. His house was nothing like the one he'd lived in while he headed up the World Police Unit, but it was a medium-sized three-bedroom brick ranch on a quiet street with a nice yard.

"You live here?" Patrick asked from around his straw.

"Yep. Moved to town close to ten months ago." Fisher grabbed his drink from the cup holder and the bags of food. "Come on."

He stood on the front sidewalk as Patrick slid out of the pickup and ambled toward him. Fisher couldn't help but grin as he heard Patrick slurping at the bottom of his drink. Luckily, he knew one thing he did have in his fridge was more Coke, and Patrick was welcome to every can.

CHAPTER TWO

Fisher did his best not to stare as Patrick consumed the cheeseburger and fries. He offered the thin man the extra burger he'd purchased, but Patrick shook his head and rubbed his stomach.

"Actually, I'm not feeling very good right now."

Fisher should've thought about that. *Hell.* "You probably shouldn't have eaten so fast." He watched Patrick's Adam's apple move up and down when he swallowed.

"Can I use your bathroom?" Patrick asked as he stood and pushed his chair in.

Fisher leaned back and pointed toward the hall. "Second door on your left. Let me know if you need anything."

Patrick hurried from the room. Fisher had to fight himself not to follow the younger man. Instead, he reached for the phone.

"Hello?" Jensen panted.

"Christ. Don't tell me the two of you are at it again?"

"Jealous?" Jensen chuckled.

"Maybe, but that's beside the point. I need to talk to your significant other."

"Why? You're not planning to drag him into your ghost hunt are you? Because I've made my feelings on that subject quite clear," Jensen snapped.

Fisher smiled as he popped two pieces of bread in the toaster. He knew Jensen wasn't lashing out at him personally. It was the fear of something happening to the man he loved that scared Jensen to the bone. "Just a few questions, promise."

Jensen sighed heavily into the phone. "Hold on."

"Hey, Fisher," Brian answered.

"Sorry for interrupting, but I have a couple things I need to talk to you about." Fisher glanced toward the hall to make sure Patrick hadn't reappeared before continuing. "Have you ever heard of a ghost that only shows himself in mirrors?"

Brian's quick intake of breath said it all. "Is that what the kid told you?"

"Yeah, but he's not really a kid, he's in his early twenties." Fisher felt the need to clarify. He dug the butter out of the refrigerator and prepared two pieces of toast to help settle Patrick's stomach. "Patrick said the only time he can see the ghost that's hurting him is in the mirror, but he also said sometimes the face changes."

"It's not a ghost. It's what we call a living spirit."

"What the hell does that mean?"

"Hang on. I'll get my granddad's journal."

Fisher heard movement on the other end of the phone and the unmistakable sound of mattress springs. If Brian was getting out of bed, Jensen was probably seething.

While Brian rustled around, Fisher finally gave in to his desire to make sure Patrick was okay. He stood and walked to the closed bathroom door. "I made you a couple pieces of toast. I think it'll settle your stomach."

"Thanks. Umm, can I use some of your toothpaste?" Patrick asked from the other side.

"Sure. There might be an extra brush in the drawer as well."

"You still there?" Brian asked.

Fisher moved away from the bathroom and traveled back to the kitchen. "I'm here."

"Okay. According to Granddad's journal, a living spirit is created by choosing to cross over."

Fisher rolled his eyes. He loved Brian, but the man seemed to think everyone knew about the paranormal. "Sorry. I still don't know what you're talking about."

Fisher heard that little clicking sound that Brian did with his tongue when he was thinking. "Well, most ghosts are created when people die, right?"

"Yeah." Fisher shook his head. *Duh.*

"Okay, so ghosts are created when people either refuse to believe they're dead or when they have some crazy need to seek vengeance for their death. With me so far?"

Fisher heard the bathroom door open moments before Patrick resumed his seat at the table. "Yeah," he answered Brian.

"Good. Now, a living spirit is not a ghost, per se. It's created when a person chooses to cross over into the spirit world of their own accord. Usually after some sort of ritual."

Fisher wondered if Patrick's father had performed such a ritual before he'd committed suicide. He wanted to ask Brian, but with Patrick sitting across from him, he knew it wasn't the right time.

"Ummm, can I call you back?" Fisher asked as he slid the plate of toast across to Patrick.

"This really isn't something you should be messing with, Fisher." .

"Yeah, well, I don't think I have much choice. See what else you can find out, and I'll talk to you later."

"Is he there with you?" Brian asked.

"Yeah." Even though Fisher wasn't looking at Patrick, he could feel the younger man's eyes on him.

"Do you want me to come down there?" Brian asked.

Fisher heard Jensen's protest in the background, and for once, he agreed with his old friend. "No. I'll call you later."

"Sooner rather than later. Living spirits are bad motherfuckers. They're not only unpredictable, but they've usually got a hidden agenda. There's a reason the person chose to cross over."

"Yeah, I get that. Thanks for the information." Fisher hung up before Brian could say anything further. As he set the phone on the table, he noticed the gooseflesh on his forearm.

"You feeling okay?" he asked Patrick.

Patrick's handsome face turned a sweet shade of pink. "I think you were right about eating too fast, but I feel better now." Patrick took a small bite. "If you want to take me home, I'll understand."

Fisher decided it would be best to tell Patrick about Brian. "I was just talking to that ex-parapsychologist friend of mine."

"Did you tell him about me?" Patrick asked before breaking off another piece of toast.

"Some."

"Does he think I'm crazy?"

"Of course not." Fisher stood and went around the table to kneel beside Patrick. "I'll try my best to protect you, but Brian's the one who can really help you."

The blue of the younger man's eyes overwhelmed Fisher. He wasn't sure if the color would be as intense if not surrounded by the long, curling, black lashes, but the effect was breathtaking.

"Does this friend of yours think he can help me?"

Fisher's gaze shifted focus from Patrick's eyes to his sensual mouth. He wondered if the plumpness to the rose-colored lips was caused by the healing cut or if they were naturally that way.

"I need to figure out a way for the two of you to talk. Jensen, his partner, won't let him come here."

"He's gay?"

Fisher nodded. "I tend to surround myself with friends who're like me. Does that bother you?"

Patrick's pink tongue began licking at a crumb that clung to his lip. Fisher barely managed to suppress a groan. He knew Patrick had no idea what that tongue was doing to him.

"Is it natural?" Patrick finally asked.

"Is what natural, being gay?"

Patrick nodded. "My father used to taunt me with it. He told me the reason he did the stuff he did was to make me hate men. He wanted me to find a woman and have children, but I've never thought of women that way." Patrick's soft voice began to lull Fisher toward him.

Although he knew it was wrong, Fisher couldn't stop thinking about the lips so close to his own. "Have you always been attracted to men?" he asked.

Patrick shrugged. "I used to, like, look at pictures and stuff. But I haven't done anything like that since…"

"Since your dad started his late-night visits," Fisher finished for him.

Patrick nodded. "I didn't think it would feel like that. I guess I was pretty naïve to think I'd like it."

Fisher reached out and cupped Patrick's cheek. "There's a world of difference between what your father's been doing to you and making love with someone you care about."

Patrick rubbed his cheek against Fisher's palm. "Will you make love to me?"

The question snapped Fisher out of the dream world he'd escaped to. He pulled back and released his hold on Patrick. "I can't."

Patrick's expression reminded Fisher of a kicked puppy. "Why?"

"Because you're too young for me and you wouldn't be doing it for the right reasons." Fisher was positive that Patrick had no idea what the refusal had cost him. It wasn't often that Fisher turned down a roll in the sack with a good-looking man, but he knew Patrick was in no position to start a sexual relationship. Who knew the kind of emotional damage years of abuse had taken on the younger man.

Patrick lifted his hands to his head. When the long, slender fingers connected with the stubble there, he dropped them again. "What would be the right reason?"

Fisher didn't feel like getting into this discussion. It had been hard enough to turn down Patrick's offer the first time. He wasn't sure that he'd be strong enough to do it again. "You'll know when it's right."

Patrick's gaze flicked to look out the window. "So what do we do now?"

Getting to his feet, Fisher started clearing away the remains of their dinner. There was still half a piece of toast left on Patrick's plate, but he decided to let it go since Patrick no longer seemed hungry. "Well, we can watch a movie, or sit out on the back deck. Of course if you're tired, I can always show you to the guest room and you can turn in early tonight."

"A movie would be nice, but I'm not sure I could concentrate."

"It's a beautiful evening. We could crack open a few beers and watch the sun set." Fisher offered.

Patrick stood and pushed his chair in. When he turned toward him, Fisher couldn't help but notice the bulge behind the zipper of Patrick's faded, dirty jeans. Fisher spun around and opened the fridge, afraid his own cock would react to seeing an aroused Patrick.

He grabbed two bottles of beer and passed one to Patrick before opening the back door. "I have other things to drink if you think beer will be too much for your stomach."

"Beer's fine," Patrick replied.

The deck was Fisher's oasis. He'd spent a hell of a lot of money to build the large deck that ran the length of his house. He'd even had a roof put overhead so he could enjoy the view rain or shine. He switched on the outdoor ceiling fans and gestured toward one of the deep pieces of furniture.

Fisher grinned when Patrick chose his favorite lounger. Covered in a deep red fabric, the lounger resembled a large round bed more than a sofa, but it did have a short back on it with colorful yellow and red floral-print pillows.

Fisher took a swig of his beer and settled into the matching chair opposite Patrick. After setting his beer on the end table, he untied his boots and pulled them off, setting them on the floor beside the footstool.

"I like your ring," Patrick said, pointing to the large diamond and ruby signet ring on Fisher's right finger.

"Thanks. It was my father's." Fisher had worn the heirloom so long he rarely noticed it.

"It's cool." Patrick removed his worn sneakers. He bit his lip as he studied the large hole in the toe of his sock, finally deciding to pull them off as well. "This is really nice," Patrick said, sitting stiffly on the sofa-bed.

"It is," Fisher agreed. "The furniture's for living, so make yourself comfortable."

Patrick smiled and settled into the profusion of pillows with a sigh. "I bet you have a lot of parties out here."

"Nope. Actually, you're the first person to visit my house besides the widow next door who came over to drop off a pie when I first moved in." Fisher picked up his beer and took another drink.

He watched as Patrick took a sip of his beer. The younger man's facial expression told him a few things. "Don't like beer?" Fisher guessed.

Patrick shrugged and took another sip. "Never had it before. I think it must be an acquired taste."

Fisher chuckled and finished off his bottle. "Well I'm gonna get me another. Would you rather have a Coke?"

"Yes, please."

Fisher started to reach for Patrick's beer, but the younger man shook his head. "I'll finish it. Wouldn't be right to waste it."

"You don't have to."

"Yeah, I do. You've been nicer to me than anyone I've ever met. Wouldn't be right if I didn't."

Fisher could tell by the look in Patrick's eyes that he was serious. Fisher's heart melted a little more. *So damn young*. He turned and retreated into the house before he got himself into trouble. He tossed the empty bottle into the recycle bin and opened the fridge. He stood there longer than necessary, hoping the air would cool his overheated body.

He continued to remind himself that he was supposed to be helping Patrick, lusting after the man's small, lean body wasn't part of it. Patrick's earlier offer made it that much harder for Fisher to keep his hands to himself. He tried to remember what the guy had been through at the hands of his father. No. Sex with Patrick was out of the question.

Fisher grabbed another beer and a can of Coke and returned to the deck. The sun was slipping lower in the sky, washing the deck in a warm glow of gold light. He turned his attention to Patrick and held out the cold red can. It was then that he noticed Patrick's closed eyes.

Fisher went around to the other side of the sofa to get a better look at the sleeping man. Had anyone ever looked more beautiful in sleep? Fisher doubted it was even possible. He was transfixed by the play of light against Patrick's skin. In the darkening light of the evening, Patrick's bruises all but faded away.

Without thought, Fisher sat on the edge of the large round cushion and watched the younger man sleep. No longer did the sunset hold its appeal. Nothing could have compared to Patrick Donnelly in that moment.

He wished he knew what it was about Patrick that had so enraptured him. Maybe it was loneliness? Even though he'd tried time and time again, Fisher knew he just didn't fit in with the rest of the locals. He'd been to the picnics, the free concerts in the park, hell, he'd even tried going to the local beer joint a time or two. None of it had made a difference. If folks took the time to talk to him, Fisher always got the feeling they were sizing him up. He'd wondered if it was the color of his skin or the size of his build.

Fisher laid his head down on the stack of pillows beside Patrick's. He was within six inches of the man's face as he continued to stare at him. Would Patrick freak out if he woke up?

He couldn't help but grin. He had a feeling Patrick would open his eyes and smile. Fisher could picture those twin dimples deepening as Patrick flashed his pearly whites. The guy was a temptation he'd have to overcome. Maybe if things were different and they'd met in a bar, Fisher would've taken Patrick up on his earlier offer. Hell, who was he kidding? He'd have dragged Patrick to the bedroom so fast the guy's head would've been spinning. Within moments, Fisher would've had Patrick's jeans down around his ankles as he buried his big cock in that tight little ass. He liked to fuck hard, fast, and often when he had a willing partner, but despite Patrick's request, Fisher doubted the younger man was ready for his brand of fucking.

Fisher reached down and ran his hand across the erection pressing against his fly. *Not gonna happen, jackass.* With a sigh, he removed himself from the sofa. He knew if he stuck around and continued to watch Patrick sleep, he'd be more than tempted to throw his good intentions out the window and jump the poor man.

He happened to glance down at Patrick's shoes and socks. That's one thing he could do to keep himself busy. He knew the Walmart was still open. He picked up one of the sneakers and looked inside for a size. The entire cushioned sole was gone from the shoe. Fisher shook his head, deciding to just take the damn thing with him to match up to a new pair.

The shirt size was easily a small, but he wasn't sure about the jeans. He went back around the sofa and tried to see if there was a tag just inside the waistband. He carefully lifted the back of Patrick's T-shirt to get to the top of his jeans and gasped.

The sound woke Patrick, who immediately went into self-protection mode, swinging at the unseen person behind him. "Get away from me, you sonofabitch!"

Fisher stumbled backward, holding his hands out in front of him. "I'm sorry. I was trying to see what size you wore."

Patrick rubbed his eyes and turned to face Fisher. "Did I hurt you?"

Fisher shook his head. "You were sleeping, so I thought I'd run to Walmart and pick you up a change of clothes."

He didn't mention the bloody scratches that seemed to litter Patrick's lower back. He couldn't help wondering how far down, or up, the wounds went. One more reminder of why he couldn't touch Patrick in a sexual way.

Patrick pulled his shirt down. "I don't need anything."

Fisher sat back down and picked up the shoe he'd dropped a few minutes earlier. "I think we both know that's not true. I know you're proud, but sometimes it's okay to let someone help you."

Patrick hugged one of the pillows to his chest and buried his face in it. "Why would you want to? Why're you being so nice to me?"

Fisher couldn't even answer that question for himself. How was he supposed to explain it to Patrick?

With his face still buried in the pillow, Patrick's shoulders began to shake.

Oh hell. All the years he'd spent hardening his heart in the military and then as head of the WPU hadn't prepared him for Patrick's tears.

He reached out and rubbed the smaller man's back. "It's okay. Get it out," he said, trying to soothe.

He wished Brian was there. Brian was much better than Fisher ever thought of being at the comfort stuff. Fisher's hand curled around Patrick's shoulder and pulled the younger man to his chest.

The pillow fell to the floor as Patrick buried his face against Fisher. "I'm sorry," Patrick apologized. "I'm not usually such a baby."

Fisher used both arms to hold Patrick in a protective embrace. "I think if anyone's due for a good cry, it's you."

He wasn't sure at what point Patrick's tears started to dry up, but a soft open mouth kiss landed at the base of his throat. Fisher's eyes closed as Patrick continued to kiss his way around and up Fisher's neck.

"We shouldn't do this," Fisher only half protested.

Patrick turned and straddled Fisher's lap in one smooth move. "Kiss me," Patrick whispered against Fisher's lips.

Fisher opened his eyes and stared into the bright blue depths in front of him. *God, I'm going to hell.* He closed the distance and took Patrick's mouth in a passionate kiss. He swept the interior of Patrick's mouth with his tongue, tasting the stale beer the man had drunk earlier.

Patrick moaned and pressed his body closer to Fisher. The pressure of Patrick's weight against his cock had Fisher hard in no time. Fisher cupped the small ass in his lap with his hands and squeezed.

Patrick began rocking back and forth against Fisher's erection, and Fisher knew he was about to flip the younger man onto his back and take him right there.

He broke the kiss and shook his head. "We can't," he said, lifting Patrick off his lap.

"Why?"

Why? Fisher no longer really knew the answer to that question. He decided to go with the old standby answer. "Just trust me, okay? If something is meant to happen, it will."

Patrick didn't seem convinced, but at least he didn't push the issue. Fisher ran a hand over the botched buzz job covering Patrick's head. "Can I ask?"

Patrick ran his own hand over his head. "I got tired of being dragged around by my hair, and since I refuse to look into mirrors…" Patrick shrugged and dropped his hand to his lap. "Does it look that bad?"

Fisher doubted that anything could look bad on Patrick. "No, but you missed a couple of spots. I'll fix it in the morning if you want."

Fisher clapped his hands together, like he always did when he was ready to change the subject. The loud noise startled Patrick. "Sorry. Bad habit. Why don't you get some more rest while I run to the store and pick you up something else to wear?"

"You really don't have to do that. I'm gonna have to go home eventually. I've got stuff there."

Fisher didn't want to say anything, but from the look of Patrick's clothes, he doubted he had much at home. "We're going to do whatever we can to keep you away from whatever's hurting you. Can I ask you a question?"

Patrick nodded.

"Before he killed himself, did you ever see your dad performing rituals or anything that seemed odd to you?"

"You mean like praying?" Patrick shook his head. "My dad wasn't religious."

"Hmmm." Fisher scratched at his beard. He glanced at Patrick and realized he'd given the younger man quite a rash around his mouth. Either he was going to have to stop kissing Patrick, or shave.

He stood abruptly, trying to get the memory of Patrick's tight little body out of his mind. "Why don't you write your sizes down for me, and I'll get going."

* * * *

After Fisher left the house, Patrick ambled around the living room looking at the wall of pictures. He was impressed by the display case full of military medals. Next to the case was a photograph of a younger Fisher decked out in his United States Marine Corps uniform. *Wow.*

The man must be some kind of hero. No wonder he wasn't interested in a romp. There were several pictures of a handsome man, first standing beside Fisher in uniform and then embracing a smaller, smart-looking guy.

Patrick noticed the smudge on the glass over the handsome man's face. He leaned closer and studied the smudge. Had Fisher tried to touch the man's face through the glass? He couldn't help but wonder who the man was to Fisher. Did Fisher love him?

He tried to shake the depressing thought away. He held no claim on Fisher. Fisher was free to love whoever he chose, so why did the idea hurt so much?

Patrick spun away from the picture. He knew the answer and didn't like it. How many hours had he known Fisher? It was completely impossible to have feelings for someone in such a short time.

Another grouping of photos caught his eye, Fisher in a business suit, standing next to the President of the United States. "Fuck me." Who the hell was this guy?

An eerily familiar face appeared in the glass covering the picture. Before Patrick had time to react, he was knocked to the floor. He scrambled backward like a crab, seeking the nearest corner. The problem with getting your ass kicked by a ghost was not being able to see the blow coming.

The first lewd grope had bile rising in Patrick's throat. It didn't seem to matter if he wore clothes or was completely nude, his father's mouth and hands always felt the same.

"Please," Patrick begged. "Not here. Not now."

The unseen hands released their hold, and Patrick let out a sigh of relief. Maybe Fisher had been right and his dad didn't hold as much power away from the house he'd killed himself in.

Suddenly, one by one, the photographs began popping off the wall to fly across the room toward him. Patrick tried to shield himself, but his skinny arms offered little protection. He hissed as a shard of glass embedded itself in his forearm.

Patrick tried to concentrate on the steady drip of blood covering his jeans. He knew he couldn't stop what was about to happen. The only thing he could do was pray his father finished with him before Fisher returned.

Another blow landed against the side of his head. There were times when his father's ghost seemed mollified by beating Patrick without raping him. He took each blow, hoping if he didn't fight back, his father would get bored and move on for a while.

When he felt teeth sink into the soft skin above his groin, he knew the truth. He was going to pay for accepting Fisher's offer of friendship.

CHAPTER THREE

Fisher grabbed the plastic sacks and headed inside. He unlocked the front door and came face to face with a nightmare. His entire living room lay in shambles. Glass and broken picture frames littered the floor as well as the soft down stuffing from his sofa and chair. The most chilling sight was the words etched deep into the walls. *He's Mine!*

Fuck. "Patrick?" he called, scanning the room.

"Patrick!" he screamed, looking in every corner and behind the torn couch.

"I'm here," Patrick replied as he stepped out of the bathroom, holding a bloodied washcloth against his arm.

Fisher rushed over. He held the younger man at arm's length until he was able to assess his injuries. There were a few small cuts to the side of his face, and neck, but the wound currently being covered with the cloth appeared to be the most serious.

Sliding his arms around Patrick, Fisher thanked the heavens the young man hadn't been seriously injured. "We need to get you to a hospital."

Patrick pulled away. "No. I need you to take me home."

Fisher could see the tears still drying on Patrick's cheeks. "I won't let you go back there."

Patrick groaned as Fisher kissed the side of his neck. "He'll kill me if you don't."

Fisher continued to kiss and nuzzle Patrick's soft skin, making his way to those lips he'd tasted earlier. The fear he'd felt stepping into the destroyed room helped him make up his mind. He'd protect Patrick with his life if it came to it.

Patrick's mouth opened immediately, and Fisher thrust his tongue inside as his arms gathered the thin body against him. As their tongues dueled, their hands began to wander, each of them trying to get closer.

A hiss of pain from Patrick brought Fisher out of his sexual haze. He broke the kiss and noticed the rag on Patrick's arm was becoming blood soaked.

"Shit. We need to get you outta here," Fisher said. With an arm still wrapped around Patrick's waist, Fisher led him into the bedroom. He withdrew an expensive-looking suitcase out of the closet and tossed it on the bed. "Let me grab some clothes, and I'll get you to the hospital."

"I don't need a hospital, just a needle and some fishing line. I have a big spool of it at home."

Fisher stopped in the process of throwing shirts into a suitcase. "Please don't tell me you've stitched yourself up before."

Patrick shrugged. "Easier than being made fun of at the hospital. Besides, I don't have the money…"

Fisher stopped him with a kiss. "This isn't about money. I know you don't have any, and I don't care."

When it didn't appear Patrick was going to argue, Fisher continued packing his bag. He threw his shaving kit on top of his clothes along with his gun. Patrick stared at the gun and began to shift uncomfortably.

"Does it bother you?" Fisher asked.

Patrick glanced up from the gun and nodded. Fisher knew he needed to talk to Patrick about it, but the need to get out of the house was greater. He closed his suitcase and lifted it from the bed.

"Come on. We can talk on the way."

* * * *

Patrick couldn't believe how nice the doctor was who had stitched his arm. He wasn't sure what story Fisher had given the emergency room staff, but they didn't treat him like he was delusional. It was quite a change from the Hickory County Hospital in town, which he'd gone to in the past.

"You're all set," Fisher said, coming into the room.

Patrick slid off the narrow bed. "Are you taking me home now?"

Fisher shook his head. "I told you, I'm never taking you back there." He ushered Patrick out of the small exam room and down the hall. "I called in a few favors."

"For what?" Patrick asked as they left the hospital and headed toward Fisher's truck.

"A place to stay and a way to get there." Fisher unlocked the passenger door and helped Patrick inside. A few seconds later, he climbed behind the wheel. "I used to head up the WPU."

"WPU?" Patrick fastened his seat belt.

"World Police Unit."

"And you're working as a deputy for Hickory County?" Patrick questioned.

"Long story, but the point is I know a lot of very powerful people. One of whom owes me his life. Sal has agreed to help, but I didn't tell him the full truth. I figured I'd do that once we got there."

"Where?" Patrick had never been far from home, so he had no real idea of how long it would take before his father caught up with him.

"Pont-Aven, France." Fisher turned onto the interstate heading east. "I hope we'll have more time to figure this whole thing out if we put an ocean between us and your father."

Patrick turned to stare out of the passenger window. He knew Fisher was just trying to help, but the farther they traveled from home, the more nervous he became. He glanced down at the athletic shoes Fisher had purchased. They were the nicest shoes he'd ever worn, not to mention the jeans, T-shirt, and hoodie that Fisher had also bought for him.

"How do we get there?"

"Private plane." Fisher reached over and touched Patrick's thigh. "Are you nervous?"

"Yeah." Patrick traced several scars on Fisher's big black hand before fingering the ring Fisher never took off. "I can't pay you back."

"Didn't ask you to." Fisher glanced at Patrick before returning his eyes to the highway. "I retired from the WPU because I was tired of the bureaucratic bullshit, but I still wanted to help keep people safe. I thought the job with the sheriff's department would do that, but I haven't felt at home, or that I was making a difference." He turned his hand over and threaded his fingers through Patrick's. "I believe some unknown entity sent me to Hickory County to help you."

"You mean like God?" Patrick asked. "Do you really believe he cares about me?" He'd given up on God years earlier, after the death of his mother when he was a kid. The years following only cemented his belief that God no longer cared about abused kids in Arkansas. Or maybe it was just him that had been forsaken.

"I've seen firsthand what comes out of hell. It only makes sense that something good is also out there."

"My dad used to say that my grandpa was the devil." Patrick lifted their clasped hands to his face and rubbed the back of Fisher's against his cheek. "I went to see him once when I was around eight. It wasn't too long before he died."

"And was he the devil?"

"He had cold eyes and he kept looking at me like he already knew how I'd turn out. He had a tube down his throat, so he couldn't say anything, but I'll never forget those eyes." Patrick rubbed Fisher's knuckles across his lips. "The same eyes my dad had before he killed himself."

"Your grandpa died of natural causes, though, right?" Fisher turned into a small regional airport.

"Not really. He yanked his breathing tube out and suffocated himself." The moment they parked, Patrick unfastened his seat belt and slid over next to Fisher. He wrapped his arms around Fisher and held on. "I don't have a passport," he mumbled.

"Like I said, I know a lot of powerful people." Fisher tilted Patrick's chin up and kissed him. He eventually pulled back enough to stare down at Patrick. "We'll figure this out. I just need you to trust me."

The last person Patrick had trusted was his mom, but he still remembered that feeling of safety she had given him, and he yearned for it again. "I'm trying."

"I can't ask for more than that." Fisher leaned in and brushed his lips across Patrick's. "We're going to take a small plane to New York, but there we'll pick up a bigger one. Okay?"

"You're sitting next to me, right?"

"Absolutely. From now on, I don't want you any farther than an arm's length away."

* * * *

After arriving in New York, Fisher ushered Patrick onto a luxurious plane that was vastly different from the commercial airline they'd flown in on. He had no idea who Sal had borrowed it from or what he'd had to promise in return, but he'd bet it hadn't come cheap. He grinned, thinking of his old friend. Sal had always had a way with men and women. Despite being one of the most dangerous men Fisher had ever known, Sal could have his pick of fucks, had even had Fisher once or twice over the years. Sal's lethal edge seemed to work as an aphrodisiac to anyone he came into contact with.

"Where do I sit?" Patrick asked.

"Take your pick, although we should wait until the plane takes off and reaches altitude before we try out the couch." *Or the bedroom*, he silently added.

Patrick sat by the window. "I'm not worried this time," he said.

"Too bad." Fisher sat next to Patrick. "Does that mean you don't want me to hold you for the next seven hours?"

Patrick leaned against Fisher. "Of course I want you to hold me, but it has nothing to do with being nervous."

Fisher lifted the armrest between the seats and settled Patrick in his arms as the plane took off. The two of them hadn't slept, other than a few hours on the flight to New York, and soon he heard a soft snore coming from Patrick.

Fisher leaned his head back and closed his eyes. He tried to relax enough to drift off, but he'd never been the kind of person who could sleep in a chair. *Damn.* Making a decision, he unbuckled his seat belt before reaching for Patrick's. He lifted the sleeping man and headed to the back of the plane.

Patrick stirred when Fisher laid him on the king-sized bed. "Where are we?" he asked, rubbing his eyes.

"Still on the plane." Fisher untied Patrick's shoelaces and eased the athletic shoes off and onto the floor. "Sleep."

Patrick unzipped his new jeans and began to push them down. "A little help?"

Against his better judgment, Fisher tugged the denim down Patrick's thin, bruised legs. "Where's the underwear I bought?"

"In the bag." Patrick grinned and lifted the T-shirt off over his head.

Fisher's breath hitched. *Fuck.* Despite the bruises, scratches, and teeth marks marring the alabaster skin, Patrick's body was perfection. Obviously, the years of fighting for his life had toned his thin body in ways a gym never could.

"Jesus Christ."

Patrick's brow furrowed as he quickly reached for his discarded shirt. "They don't hurt."

Pulling the shirt from Patrick's hands, Fisher sat on the edge of the bed. "Please don't." He ran his palm across Patrick's chest to circle the scarred nipple with his fingertip. The stark contrast in their skin color reminded him of how opposite the two of them were.

"It's gross," Patrick mumbled.

"So why do I want to taste it?" Fisher followed his words with action as he leaned over to kiss and lick the small light brown disk. He was twice Patrick's age and three times his size, but Fisher was too weak to resist. He kissed his way down Patrick's chest to the perfect set of teeth marks above his cock. It was a stark reminder of what Patrick had gone through only a few hours earlier. After kissing the bruise, he sat up. "We should both get some sleep."

Fisher stood and helped Patrick get under the covers. "You need a bottle of water or anything?"

"Sure," Patrick mumbled.

Fisher braced his hands on the mattress and leaned over to give Patrick a deep kiss. "I want you, but I need you to want me."

"I do want you. I practically throw myself at you every chance I get." Patrick rolled to his side.

"I'm the first person who's ever reached out to help you. Christ, Patrick, I'm more than twice your age. I'm worried that you're so starved for compassion that you want me simply because I'm here." *Wow.* Fisher couldn't believe he'd spilled his guts like that. He wasn't used to admitting self-doubt to others. Even Jensen thought he was really the tough bastard he portrayed himself to be. "Besides, with everything you've been through, you deserve more than a dip and stir."

"Dip and stir?" Patrick questioned.

"Quick fuck," Fisher clarified.

"I'm not a girl. I don't need wine and roses, just someone who doesn't bite and beat the shit out of me."

Fisher took a step toward the door. "That's what I'm afraid of."

* * * *

After a quick, no-nonsense greeting from Sal, Fisher and Patrick climbed into the black Land Rover. Fisher decided to put some distance between him and Patrick so he chose to sit up front beside Sal while Patrick sat in back.

"This is Pont-Aven?" Patrick asked as they drove through town.

"Yes, the most beautiful place on earth," Sal answered. "Artists come from all over the world to paint the buildings and landscapes."

"I've never seen anything like it," Patrick replied.

The thick emotion in Patrick's voice caught Fisher's attention. He turned in his seat and looked back. Tears were streaming down Patrick's face. "Hey, you okay?" Fisher asked.

Patrick glanced away from the view to meet Fisher's gaze. "I'm glad I got a chance to see this before he kills me."

Shit. "Pull over for a second," Fisher told Sal.

Sal did as asked, and Fisher climbed into the backseat with Patrick. The awkwardness between them was gone in a heartbeat as Fisher wrapped his arms around the younger man.

"You're not going to die."

"My home is impenetrable," Sal said, sounding offended.

Fisher hadn't discussed the danger to Patrick over the phone with Sal. He preferred to look someone in the eyes when he told them of the existence of ghosts.

Forced to soothe both men, Fisher thumped Sal on the shoulder. "Patrick's had a rough time of it the last few years."

"No offense meant, sir." Patrick squeezed Fisher's hand and returned his attention back to the view.

Sal turned onto a wooded, winding road. "My house is the only place on the planet where I know I'm safe. You'll see."

Fisher hated to take Sal's sense of wellbeing from him, but his old friend would soon discover a completely new enemy. The Land Rover slowed as it neared a tall, chain-link fence. Sal pulled out his cell phone and punched a series of numbers into the keypad.

Shaking his head, Fisher chuckled. "You always did love your toys."

Sal glanced in the rearview mirror. "This is nothing."

In the next ten minutes, they passed through another three gates before Fisher got his first look at Sal's home. Never in a million years would he expect Sal to live in a place like the one in front of them, a bunker, sure, but not the stunning, stone-covered home at the end of the drive.

Patrick gasped as he opened the car door. "Oh my God. It's like a fairy tale."

Fisher had to agree as he joined Patrick among the profusion of blooming flowers. He glanced over his shoulder at Sal. "It truly is a sanctuary."

Sal nodded, acknowledging Fisher's praise. "Come, let's go inside."

Fisher followed, but noticed Patrick hadn't moved. "Patrick?"

"Would it be okay if I stay out here for a few minutes?" Patrick asked.

Fisher looked at Sal who shrugged. "Sure. Just don't go near the fence."

"I won't." Patrick walked farther into the garden.

Sal preceded Fisher inside and tapped the code into the security system. "So what's the real story with the kid? You fucking him?"

Fisher walked into the living room and sat on the deep sofa. "It's complicated."

"How the fuck can it be complicated? He's too young to come with baggage," Sal argued.

"That's just it, he *is* too young and he does come with a shitload of baggage." Fisher wondered if he'd hold back if Patrick were ten years older. He seriously doubted it. He'd seen firsthand how an intense situation could bring two people closer than months of dating ever hoped to.

"If he's legal, he's not too young, so that argument doesn't fly. Does the baggage have anything to do with your frantic call to me in the middle of the night?" Sal moved the fireplace screen and squatted down, turning his back to Fisher. It said a lot about the trust the two of them had built over the years.

Fisher scowled. "I don't do frantic."

"You were ready to piss yourself when you called." Sal lit a match and touched it to the crumpled newspaper under the logs. "Don't bullshit me, Marx. I've been in some heavy-duty fucked-up situations with you and never have I heard fear in your voice like I did last night." He stood and crossed to stare out the window. "What's going on with the kid that put that fear in your voice?"

Fisher leaned forward and rested his forearms on his knees. "Do you believe in ghosts?"

Sal spun around. "You mean the creaky noises, bump in the night kind of shit?"

"No, I mean the rip-your-clothes-off-and-fuck-your-own-son kind of ghost." Fisher scrubbed his face with his palms. "Patrick's lived for years with that kind of ghost, and no one would help or believe him."

"Until you found him," Sal said, nodding in understanding.

"You're not questioning the existence of them?" Fisher asked, surprised.

Sal returned his attention to the garden, and most likely, Patrick. "No," he eventually said. He crooked his fingers. "Come here."

Confused, Fisher stood and moved to stand beside Sal. "Wh…" *Fuck.* Patrick was kneeling in the largest flower bed with his hand buried in the dirt. His eyes were closed and he appeared to be talking to himself. In a circular pattern around him, flower petals floated in the air in a whirlwind of color.

"Does that happen often?" Sal asked. "Because if it does, I'd rather he didn't wander the gardens in the back of the house."

Ashamed to admit that he didn't know, Fisher avoided the question. He crossed the living room to the front door. "Stay here," he told Sal on his way out.

Fisher stood at the edge of the garden. Although Patrick was only a few feet away, Fisher couldn't understand what he was saying. He stepped closer and realized the reason. Patrick wasn't speaking English at all. He motioned for Sal to come out of the house, hoping his friend would know the language.

Moments later, Sal stood beside him. Fisher put a finger to his lips before pointing to his ear.

Sal's eyes narrowed as he took a step closer. He pulled a cell phone from his pocket and held it out, obviously recording Patrick's odd language and speech pattern. Suddenly, Sal dropped the phone and shook his hand.

"Fuck," he hissed, blowing on his reddened palm.

Patrick's body jerked several times.

Fisher pushed Sal out of the way to get to Patrick. He knelt, crushing a few bare flower stems. "Patrick?"

Patrick's closed eyes squeezed tighter together as his speech and dialect changed completely.

Fisher felt the ground under him grow hotter until he was forced to squat instead of kneel. He reached for Patrick's forearms and tried to pull them free of the soil, but they wouldn't budge.

"Let go, Patrick!"

Patrick hands sank deeper into the ground past his wrists to his forearms. His stare was vacant as if he were in some sort of trance.

"Sal, help me." Fisher concentrated on Patrick's left arm while Sal took the right. "On the count of three. One, two, three!" He tried to pull Patrick's hand out of the dirt with every ounce of strength he had, but it only seem to sink deeper into the flower bed. "Patrick? What's happening?"

"Fuck, look at the flowers," Sal said, pointing to the dying blooms. "They're cooking."

Frustrated, Fisher tried once again to pull Patrick free as he screamed at the unseen force that held him. "He's mine, you fucker! You can't have him!"

Patrick blinked and turned his head toward Fisher. "Shhh," he whispered.

Fisher opened his mouth to argue when something slammed into him. Knocked off balance, he felt as light as a feather as he flew through the air to land ten yards away. Before he could get to his feet again, he felt a searing pain rip down his chest.

"Fucking hell!" Sal yelled as he ran to Fisher's side. He tore off his T-shirt and held it against Fisher's chest. "Shit, man. Whatever the fuck that was, it got you good."

Patrick started coughing, drawing Fisher and Sal's attention. He was wiping the dirt from his hands with a dazed expression on his face.

Despite the pain he was in, Fisher crawled across the flower bed, crushing everything that wasn't already dead. "Patrick?"

Patrick turned to stare at Fisher. "You drew him to yourself. Don't do that."

"I'm not afraid of your father," Fisher replied, wrapping his arms around Patrick.

Patrick shook his head. "That wasn't my father."

* * * *

Once they stopped the bleeding and Sal had helped Patrick get Fisher to bed, Patrick insisted he be left alone to tend Fisher's wounds. "It's okay. I know what I'm doing," Patrick said, trying to reassure Sal.

Sal stared down at Fisher. "Do you think we should take him to the hospital?"

Patrick shook his head. "I've been taking care of myself for a long time." He lifted his T-shirt and showed Sal the scars on his chest. "All except this one." He pointed to the fresh set of sutures. "Fisher took me to a nice doctor who did these for me."

"Fuck," Sal said, reaching out to touch the longest of the scars that ran down Patrick's torso. "Your father did that to you?"

"Yeah." Patrick looked Sal in the eyes. He knew if Sal was going to help, he needed to know all of it. "My father likes to draw blood."

Sal winced before breaking eye contact and staring down at Fisher once more. "I'm glad Fisher found you. Believe me, you couldn't ask for a better guy at your side."

Patrick opened the first aid box and removed a butterfly bandage. He wished Sal was a fisherman so he could have some line, but he'd make do with what he had. It wouldn't be the first time.

"Fisher's too good a man to be with someone like me, isn't he?"

"I didn't say that."

"I know, but I think it all the time." Patrick gently closed one of Fisher's wounds with the bandage. "I want him to touch me, but he won't."

"He thinks you're too young, and that you've been through too much." Sal put a hand on Patrick's shoulder. "Marx is an intense and dangerous lover. It takes a strong man to handle him."

Patrick couldn't help but laugh. "I guarantee he couldn't be half as brutal as what I'm used to," he replied. "I just want to know what it feels like to be touched for pleasure and not out of anger. I want to feel him above me, to know he's real."

Sal unfastened Fisher's jeans and pulled them down and off. He looked at Patrick before lowering Fisher's underwear. "That, my young friend, is very real, so you need to make sure you know what you're getting into."

Patrick couldn't help but stare at the large flaccid cock lying against Fisher's thigh. An involuntary moan escaped him as he imagined the cock hard and sliding in and out of him.

Sal dropped the jeans and underwear to the floor along with Fisher's boots. "Yeah, he's used to that reaction." He turned and headed for the door. "I'll go find some pain medicine. I'm sure he'll need it when he wakes up."

Left alone with Fisher, Patrick continued to stare at Fisher's body. Other than the cuts that ran across his chest, Fisher's body was absolute perfection. He slid off the bed and leaned over Fisher's cock. God, he wanted to touch it. He lowered his head until his lips brushed the bulbous head. Closing his eyes, he licked the soft skin from crown to base.

Fisher made a noise, snapping Patrick out of his sexual haze.

Patrick reared back so fast that he landed on his ass. Taking advantage of an unconscious man was bad. He shook his head and got to his feet. With shame in his heart for what he'd almost done, Patrick resumed first aid on Fisher.

* * * *

Patrick eased out of the bedroom and headed down the steps, pocketing Fisher's phone. He knew he'd have to confess to Fisher what he'd done earlier.

Sal met him in the foyer before he could make it to the door. "How is he?"

"Still sleeping." Patrick tried to go around Sal, but Sal moved to block his way.

"So where're you going?" Sal asked.

"Now that I know Fisher can get hurt, I have to do something to draw attention back to myself." The sight of Fisher's wounds had put an end to Patrick's dream of ever being free. He tried to get around Sal to the door.

"I don't think my garden can handle another walk."

"I don't think you want me in your nice house when whoever the hell attacked Fisher comes back." Patrick tried once more to get around Sal, but the dangerous-looking man refused to let him by. He had no idea what had happened in the garden, but he knew Fisher's attacker hadn't been his father. "I won't let Fisher get hurt again."

Sal stared at Patrick for several moments before holding up a phone. "I've been working on this, and there's something you need to hear." He gestured to a room Patrick had yet to explore. "Relax, it's just my office."

Patrick nodded and followed Sal into a wood-paneled room. Every electronic gadget imaginable was lined up neatly beside wall-to-wall computers. In the center of the room was a long oval table surrounded by at least ten leather chairs. He pulled out the nearest one and sat.

Sal set the phone on the glossy wooden surface and reached for Patrick's hands. "They don't even look red."

"Why should they?" Patrick asked. He had few memories from his time in the garden.

Sal shook his head and released Patrick's hands. "Nothing. Never mind." He walked over to the work area and retrieved a small handheld device. "I managed to save some of what I recorded earlier. I think you need to hear it."

Patrick stared at his hands. They looked like they always had. "What happened out there?"

"It's not important. It's probably better that you don't remember most of it. Just listen to the tape."

"Okay." Patrick prayed it wasn't a recording of him begging not to be fucked.

When Sal hit a button, a gentle voice came over the small speaker. He tried to concentrate on what was being said, but the words didn't make sense to him. "What are they saying?"

"I don't know. I thought maybe you would." Sal stared at him. "I was recording *you*. I know it doesn't sound like you, but you were the only one speaking."

Patrick's stomach roiled at the thought of yet another spirit violating him. "Is that really me?"

"Yes," Sal played the recording again. "This is the first voice you were speaking in. The second one didn't record. Do you understand anything?"

A brief memory came to mind. "I don't know what I'm saying, but it reminds me of something. A week or so before my dad killed himself, I found him in the kitchen talking like this. He was just sitting there at the table, staring into a bowl of soggy cereal. It didn't last long after I said his name, but he was under a lot of pressure and stuff, so I thought he'd just snapped."

"I hope you don't mind, but I need to understand exactly what we're dealing with if I'm going to be of any help."

Patrick nodded in understanding.

"Outside, you said the ghost who attacked Marx wasn't your father. How did you know that?"

Searching his memories, Patrick realized the awful truth. "Because it was in me first, and I know what my father feels like." Patrick rubbed his face. "The one who hurt Fisher was probably the man in the glass."

"What man?"

Patrick rubbed his temples. "I've only seen him a couple of times. I don't know who he is, but he's old and thin." He lowered his gaze. "He's been in me before."

"So your dad isn't the only spirit fucking you?" Sal asked.

Patrick wasn't used to someone who was so forward or so crass. "No, I meant I've felt him inside of me." He rubbed his chest. "I lose time once in a while, and after I wake up, I feel different, darker, if that makes sense. It usually goes away in a day or so, but it definitely isn't my father." He tried to picture the face of the man he'd seen in the glass numerous times. "And he dresses funny." He wondered if he should mention the other spirit he felt in the garden, but since the newcomer seemed peaceful, he decided it wasn't pressing at the moment.

Sal stared at the phone for several moments. "Funny how?"

Patrick shrugged. "He always wears some kind of heavy, hooded robe. Even when it's hot outside."

"I know someone who might be able to shed some light on what's going on. Not with the clothes necessarily but with the language you're speaking in that recording. My friend has shitty phone reception, though, so I'll have to go see him." He glanced at the ceiling as if he could see through it to where Fisher slept. "I hate to leave Marx alone, but I'm sure Gavin'll want to speak with you."

"Maybe we should wait until Fisher wakes up," Patrick suggested. He didn't like the idea of leaving Fisher alone. What if his father or the other bad spirit decided to take their anger out on Fisher? Patrick shook his head. "No. I can't leave him alone until he can take care of himself. He wouldn't do it to me, and I can't do it to him."

"I can't help either of you until I figure out what the hell is going on. In order to do that, I need to see my friend," Sal explained again.

Patrick wasn't accustomed to defying people, and Sal looked like he could kick ass without breaking a sweat, but… "I'm sorry," he mumbled. "I'll go with you tomorrow, but today I'm going to sit outside in case that thing comes back."

Sal paced back and forth in front of his desk. "Sit for a while on the stone bench in the gazebo." He glanced over his shoulder and stared at Patrick. "Away from my flowers. But be back inside once the sun sets."

"Why? Are there animals that come out at night?"

Sal shook his head. "No, but if Marx finds out I let you sit out there all night, I'll have to fight him, and I really don't want to do that again."

CHAPTER FOUR

"Fisher?"

Fisher heard his name but didn't open his eyes until he felt the warm touch of a hand on his shoulder. He smiled at Patrick. "Hey."

Patrick gestured to a tray of food on the bedside table. "Are you hungry? I brought you some soup."

Fisher stared up at Patrick. He couldn't remember the last time someone cared enough to look after him. "I could eat something." He held his bandaged chest as he moved to rest his back against the antique headboard. "What time is it?"

"Almost eight." Patrick settled the tray on Fisher's lap. "I hope you like vegetable. I thought about chicken noodle, but I didn't have enough time to make the noodles and I didn't want to leave and go to the store."

"Vegetable is great," Fisher replied. Truth was, he hated vegetables, always had. Corn was okay, and potatoes, but potatoes weren't really a vegetable, so he doubted they counted. He reached for Patrick but only managed to graze the younger man's hip as he rose quickly off the bed. "Is something wrong?"

Patrick flushed but shook his head. "I'm fine." He opened a bottle of pills and shook out three. "You need to take these with your dinner." He set the pills on the corner of the table instead of handing them to Fisher.

The longer Fisher watched Patrick, the more he became convinced something was wrong. "Where's Sal?"

"Downstairs. I think he's mad at me."

"Why would he be mad?" Fisher prepared to move his tray to the side. If Sal had tried to seduce Patrick, he'd kill the bastard.

"Sal wanted me to go with him to talk to someone who might be able to help me, but I couldn't leave you here alone," Patrick explained.

Fisher knew Sal wouldn't have shown his anger unless something else had happened. "Would you do me a favor and tell Sal I'd like to speak to him?"

Patrick's dark eyebrows drew together. "You're not gonna yell at him, are you?"

Fisher gave Patrick a gentle smile. "No. I want to know more about this friend of his," he lied. "Would you mind if I spoke to him alone for a few minutes?"

Patrick shook his head but didn't meet Fisher's gaze. He shuffled his feet for a few moments before digging in his pocket.

Producing Fisher's cell phone, he cleared his throat. "I'm sorry. This rang earlier, but I didn't want it to wake you up, so I took it." He handed the phone to Fisher. "You've had a couple of calls, but I didn't answer them," he said in a rush.

Although Fisher was anxious to go through his missed calls, he set the phone down and beckoned Patrick. "Come here."

It took a moment, but eventually, Patrick moved toward the bed. He sat gingerly on the mattress beside Fisher. "Are you mad at me for what happened to you?"

"Why would I be angry with you?" Fisher set the tray on the bedside table and held out his arms. He was more than pleased when Patrick accepted the invitation.

"I don't want to hurt you."

"You won't." Fisher was willing to suffer a little discomfort to hold and reassure Patrick.

Patrick snuggled against Fisher's chest, obviously taking care to avoid the fresh cuts. He kissed Fisher's neck while pushing his hand under the blanket to Fisher's groin.

Fisher thought about stopping Patrick as the younger man ran his hand down the length of his hardening cock, but couldn't bring himself to refuse Patrick's touch. "You don't have to do that."

"I want to," Patrick replied. "I have to tell you something, but I'm afraid of what you'll say when I do."

"I doubt there's much you can say that'll make me mad, unless you tell me you let Sal put his hands on you while I slept." The thought of Sal stealing Patrick away from him made his gut clench.

Patrick shook his head. "Sal didn't touch me, but he took your clothes off and showed me your dick."

Surprised, Fisher scooted down in bed until his head rested on the pillow. "Did you enjoy looking at me?"

Patrick bit his lip. "Yeah. Yours is a lot bigger than mine."

"Mine's a lot bigger than most." Fisher kissed Patrick softly on the lips several times before delving his tongue inside. Christ, he loved the way Patrick accepted his kisses. Despite everything Patrick had gone through, he never once held back with Fisher. It was obvious that Patrick felt some affection for him, but Fisher wasn't sure if it was enough to justify making love to the younger man. *Hell.* He groaned when Patrick's long fingers wrapped around his erection. "Feels good," he moaned.

"Can I taste you?" Patrick asked.

Fisher yanked the blanket off and tossed it to the floor. He was tired of being the good guy. "Babe, you can do anything you want to me."

Patrick sat up and stared down at Fisher's cock for several seconds. "You say that, but every time I ask you to fuck me, you turn me down." He bent over and swiped the head of Fisher's cock with his tongue. "Sal said it's because I'm too young and weak. He told me you like to fuck hard."

Fisher settled his hand on the back of Patrick's head. It was amazing how large his hand looked in comparison. "Sal shouldn't have told you that."

Patrick wrapped his lips around the crown of Fisher's cock for several moments before pulling back. "I don't really know what I'm doing."

"You're doing fine." Fisher guided Patrick down again. "Just imagine your own cock and what would make you feel good." He promised himself he'd show Patrick exactly how good it could feel once he felt better, but for the moment, he closed his eyes and let Patrick lick, suck, and thoroughly explore his cock.

A loud crack rent the air, bringing Fisher out of his sexual haze. His eyes sprang open as he jackknifed to a sitting position. Focusing in on a long fissure in the mirror attached to the antique dressing table, Fisher saw a dark robed figure in the glass moments before Patrick flew through the air.

Patrick's body made a sickening thud against the plaster wall before sliding to the floor.

"You, fucker, stay away from him!" Fisher screamed as he jumped out of bed and rushed toward the dazed younger man.

"Go!" Patrick yelled.

"I'm not leaving you," Fisher argued. He slid his arms under Patrick's knees and arms and lifted him off the floor.

Unseen hands tried to yank Patrick away from Fisher, but Fisher refused to relinquish his hold. "Sal! Get up here!"

Patrick stared up at Fisher. "You can't beat him," he whispered. "He won't let you have me."

"We'll see about that." Fisher had absolutely no idea what kind of spirit he was dealing with or how to send the fucker back to hell where it belonged. He glanced at his phone on the bed. There was no way he could get to the phone while fighting off Patrick's attacker.

"What the fuck is going…," Sal's voice dropped off as he entered the room.

"Grab my phone and help me get Patrick out of here," Fisher ordered.

Patrick cried out as his shirt was ripped from his body.

"No!" Fisher growled. "He's mine." He tried to spin away from the unseen hands raking across Patrick's thin, already scarred chest.

Sal pressed against Fisher, sandwiching Patrick between them. "Head for the door," Sal instructed.

As one, Fisher and Sal tried to protect Patrick from the flying debris as they made their way out of the room. They were almost to the staircase when Sal's legs buckled.

Fisher opened his mouth to ask Sal what the hell was going on when he saw the rivulet of blood running down the side of Sal's face from under his hairline. *Shit.* Sal had been hit.

"Put me down," Patrick demanded. "I can run faster than the two of you can carry me like this."

Fisher met Sal's gaze. He knew Patrick was telling the truth, but he also suspected it was Patrick's way of saving him and Sal from more harm. "Slide down the steps," he told Patrick. "If you try to run down them, you'll get knocked on your ass or worse."

Patrick nodded as Fisher and Sal lowered him to the ground. "Are you okay?" Fisher asked Sal.

"Don't worry about me," Sal assured him. "Let's just get the hell out of here."

Keeping as low to the steps as possible, Fisher followed Patrick down the staircase. Five feet from the door, the front windows imploded, hurtling shards of glass through the air. Instinctively, Fisher threw up his arm at the sound, covering his face from the worst of it.

Patrick's scream spurred Fisher into action. Despite the glass embedded in his chest, arms, and legs, he slid down the steps to Patrick's side. After a quick assessment of the damage, he removed several of the biggest shards. Sweeping Patrick into his arms, he raced for the door, heedless of what might be thrown at him next.

"You alive?"

Bleeding from dozens of wounds, Sal ran ahead of them to the SUV and threw open the door. "The recording," Sal said, taking off at a run back toward his office.

"Leave it!" Fisher yelled. He didn't waste time loading Patrick into the back of the SUV. He slammed the door and cradled Patrick in his lap. Despite the blood on his own shaking hands, he tried to determine which slivers could be removed from Patrick's face and chest without causing more damage. "Talk to me," he urged when he realized Patrick hadn't uttered a word.

Patrick stared up at Fisher as Sal climbed into the vehicle. "He's really pissed," Patrick mumbled.

Fisher plucked a piece of glass from Patrick's neck before tossing it out the open window. They were running out of time. "Did you get it?" he asked Sal.

"Yes. I'll head to Gavin's."

It was bad enough that he'd put Sal in a dangerous position, but how could he drag someone else into the situation? "Are you sure that's a good idea?" he asked as he pulled more glass from Patrick's body. Patrick continued to stare up at Fisher with lifeless eyes. It was obvious the younger man was in shock, but Fisher decided it might be better that he wasn't fully aware of what was happening.

"No, but Gavin's cell doesn't get service at the church. I'll try, but I doubt he'll answer."

"Church?" Fisher questioned.

"I thought I told you? Gavin and his partner, Ian, have spent the last six years restoring an old church and attached abbey about thirty kilometers up the coast. The church was abandoned and left to crumble after the last monk passed away. According to locals, the ghosts of the monks still roam the grounds."

"So we're running toward more spirits?" Fisher shook his head. "What the hell, Sal?"

Sal shrugged. "Gavin's our best bet in finding out what we're dealing with. Besides, maybe the spirits will keep Patrick's spooks at bay long enough to figure out how the hell to vanquish them." He glanced at Fisher in the rearview mirror. "Do you have a better idea?"

Fisher shook his head.

"Let me die," Patrick whispered. His voice was so soft, Fisher barely heard him.

"What?" Fisher narrowed his gaze as he stared down at Patrick. "You think I'm going to let that happen?" He didn't say it, but he knew the amped up aggression from Patrick's father was his fault. Maybe the sonofabitch had noticed Fisher's growing feelings and had decided he'd rather see Patrick dead than loved.

Patrick reached up and pulled a piece of glass from Fisher's chin. He stared at the bloody shard. "You don't deserve this."

"And neither do you," Fisher replied.

Patrick's gaze swept over Fisher's upper torso. "You're naked."

Fisher glanced down at himself and grinned. "I guess I am." He'd been so hell-bent on getting Patrick out of the house, he hadn't even noticed. His entire body hurt, so it was hard to pinpoint any one cut, but a thought occurred to him. He gently urged Patrick into a sitting position before checking out his own cock and balls. Despite a few nicks, everything appeared to be intact. There was one piece of glass sticking out of his hip, which he suspected might be a problem, but for the most part, because he'd brought up the rear on their way down the steps, Sal and Patrick had shielded him from the worst of it.

While Fisher waited for Sal to get off the phone, he plucked and shook the glass free from his hands and arms and threw them out the window. The memory of the man in the cracked mirror came to mind as he worked.

"I saw a man in the mirror who wasn't your father," he told Patrick.

Patrick nodded. "That doesn't surprise me. The man in the mirror is never my father, but he likes to watch when my dad does stuff to me. That's when I know the worst of it is about to happen."

"So you know there are two spirits haunting you, right?" Fisher asked.

"Two or two hundred, it doesn't really matter, does it? The fact is, I'm not going to make it out of this alive, and if you continue to try and save me, you won't either." Patrick followed Fisher's lead and began to remove shards from his body. As he worked, his clothes became increasingly soaked with blood.

Fisher turned to stare out the open window. As soon as he could get a moment of privacy, he needed to call Brian.

Sal ended the call. "I managed to catch Gavin while he was in town picking up supplies. He's agreed to help."

"No," Patrick said.

"Yes," Sal argued. "He wants to. Gavin's an anthropologist. He's fascinated by ancient folklore, so he's really eating this up." Sal studied Fisher in the rearview mirror for a moment. "I'm not sure how Ian will feel about it, though."

"Gavin's partner?" Fisher asked.

"Ian's the total opposite of Gavin. Sometimes I think the only reason they're still together is their mutual love of the church and abbey. Ian does most of the restoration on the place. He's the stone mason Gavin hired right after he bought the property." Sal broke eye contact and turned his attention back to the winding road in front of him. "I'm not sure how Ian will react when we pull up looking like we do."

Fisher noticed the glass still embedded in Sal's skin in the dashboard glow. He put his hand on Sal's shoulder. "You need a doctor?"

"I'm fine. I've lived through a hell of a lot worse. Although there's a place on my side that concerns me. I told Gavin to have plenty of antiseptic and bandages on hand."

They rode the last few kilometers in silence, each of them buried in their own thoughts. "There it is," Sal announced, pointing to two large stone structures on a dark green, grassy hill. The church sat approximately two hundred yards from the edge of a cliff that overlooked the Celtic Sea.

"Wow." Fisher was amazed that people actually lived in such a place. The stone structure looked incredibly formidable in the moonlight.

"It's far from finished, but they've made great headway. They've managed to finish enough space in the abbey to be livable, but they've put their primary efforts into the church itself," Sal said, pulling to a stop in front of the abbey. "No electricity, although they have a generator to power the necessary stuff."

A door opened and two men stepped out of the abbey carrying lanterns.

Fisher glanced at Patrick. "You okay now?"

Patrick wiped at his face. Fisher hadn't even noticed that Patrick had been crying in the darkened SUV.

"Hey," he soothed. He tilted Patrick's chin up and gave him a soft kiss. "We'll get through this together."

Patrick turned away from Fisher and got out of the SUV, leaving Fisher to wonder whether Patrick would recover from the latest attack. In Fisher's mind, the sexual assaults Patrick had suffered through for years should have been more spiritually damaging to the younger man, but it appeared as though the physical attacks had left more of a mark on Patrick's soul.

* * * *

It was nearly dawn by the time Patrick finished stitching Sal's wounds. It seemed as though Sal had taken the worst of the flying glass. Although Sal had tried to downplay his injuries, several deep wounds would require a good deal of bed rest.

Patrick left Sal and entered the small rudimentary kitchen. "Where's Fisher?" he asked Ian.

With short red hair and a sprinkling of freckles across his nose and cheeks, Ian looked like the typical Scot. Patrick had learned that although Ian was of strong Scottish decent, he had been born and raised in South Carolina.

"I think he went outside to try and get a signal. It's best at the bottom of the hill for some reason." Ian lifted his mug. "Would you like some coffee?"

Patrick shook his head. "Thanks, but I'm fine." He sat at the table across from Ian. "Are you angry with me for coming?"

Ian stared into the steaming coffee for several moments before answering. "You're the first person who's cared to ask that question."

"Well, to be fair, Sal's too hurt to think of much else right now, and Fisher's in protection-mode. Everything that's happened is my fault, so I should be the one to apologize for bringing this to your home."

Ian shook his head. "It's not my home. It's Gavin's."

"Oh, I'm sorry, I must've misunderstood. I thought the two of you were together." Patrick knew he'd heard Sal call Ian Gavin's partner, but maybe it meant something different in France.

Ian chuckled, but it wasn't a happy sound. "We fuck, but we're definitely not on equal footing in the relationship. Gavin's let me know on more than one occasion that this place belongs to him." He stood and walked over to the wood-burning stove to refill his cup. "Are you sure you don't want some?"

Patrick had never liked the taste of coffee, but the warmth it would provide sounded good. "Okay, yeah, but just a half a cup."

Patrick watched as Ian retrieved another mug from a shelf over the sink. Although Ian was slightly built, the muscles in his arms and back were incredibly defined. It was easy to see how his work had shaped his body.

Ian set the cup on the table in front of Patrick and gestured to the small pitcher and sugar container. "I'm not sure how you like it, so help yourself."

Patrick doctored his coffee while trying to decide how to proceed. "You don't seem very happy here, so why do you stay?"

"I'm happy with my work," Ian replied. "Pay no attention to me. Gavin's a lot to handle sometimes, but we get on well together. I didn't mean to make it sound like he's a tyrant or anything."

"You didn't." Patrick sipped the coffee. He'd put so much milk and sugar into the bitter brew that it tasted more like candy than coffee. Mmmm, just the way he liked it.

"What about Sal, is he going to be okay?" Ian asked.

"I think so. The piece of glass Fisher pulled out of his side was long and deep, but I don't think it did any permanent damage. He'll have new scars to add to the ones he already has, but unless they become infected, he should be fine." Patrick leaned on the table, using his hand to help prop his chin up. "I think Sal has more scars than I do, which is hard to believe."

Fisher walked into the room and stopped beside Patrick. "How's Sal?" he asked, putting his hand on Patrick's shoulder.

Patrick leaned his cheek against Fisher's bandaged hand. "He's sleeping. I'm worried about infection, but I think if I can keep the wounds clean enough, he'll be okay."

"I can help with that," Ian offered.

Patrick yawned. "Thanks. I'd appreciate it."

"Let's get you to bed for a few hours," Fisher suggested. "Jensen and Brian should be here sometime tonight."

"They're coming?" Patrick got to his feet after finishing his coffee. It said a lot that Fisher was willing to bring his best friend into such a dangerous situation.

"It wasn't my idea." Fisher took the cup out of Patrick's hand and carried it to the sink. "Once Brian sets his mind to something, there's no stopping him, and no way in hell would Jensen allow Brian to come alone."

"I'm sorry," Patrick said.

"I wish you'd stop saying that!" Fisher snapped harshly, prompting Patrick to raise his arms in a defensive stance. "Fuck." Fisher pulled Patrick into his arms. "I didn't mean to yell at you." He kissed the top of Patrick's head. "I just can't stand that you keep apologizing for something you have no control over, and I have no idea how to make you understand that."

Embarrassed that the exchange had happened in front of Ian, Patrick nodded and pulled out of Fisher's embrace. "I think you're right. I'm tired."

"I'm sorry, but we've only restored two of the bedrooms, so you'll have to pick one of the others. They're relatively clean, and the floor's been repaired, but that's about as far as we've gone with them." He got up and retrieved a broom from the corner of the kitchen. "You'll need this, and we're out of beds, so I set a stack of blankets on the table in the hall. Sorry, but you'll have to make a pallet with them," Ian said.

"Thanks. We'll be fine."

"If it starts to rain, there's a stack of buckets at the end of the hall for leaks," Ian told them as they left the kitchen.

Patrick carried the broom down the hall. He stopped at Sal's room to check on him. He noticed Gavin sitting at Sal's bedside, pouring over an old book. Patrick wondered whether there was anything in the antique volume that could help. With a silent sigh, he continued down the hall as Fisher gathered the blankets and single pillow. It seemed they'd be sharing, which was fine with Patrick.

"Which one?" he asked.

"Go on down," Fisher said, catching up with Patrick.

A strange pull guided him down the hall toward one of the doors in particular. "This one," Patrick said, pushing open the door.

The room was much smaller than the one Sal was in. Regardless, Patrick sighed. "Do you feel it?" he asked as he started to sweep the accumulated dust into a pile.

"Feel what?" Fisher asked.

Patrick paused. "It's warm." He shook his head, trying to fight back a memory of Sal's flower garden. "It's been years since I've felt warm inside."

Fisher tucked the blankets under one of his massive arms before lifting his hand to feel Patrick's forehead. "It's colder than shit. Maybe you're getting sick."

"I'm not sick." Patrick quickly swept a large enough area to make a bed. "As a matter-of-fact, I feel better than I have in years." Despite Fisher's claims, Patrick knew the warmth he felt was a good sign.

Fisher began to spread out the blankets. "Four blankets. I say we sleep on two and cover up with two. What do you think?"

"Doesn't matter." Patrick smiled and began to remove the clothes he'd borrowed from Ian. Even completely naked, he didn't feel the slightest chill in the air. He didn't want to freak Fisher out by telling him there was a protective spirit in the room, but he knew in his heart there was.

Fisher pulled a small tube of lube out of the pocket of a borrowed robe before quickly getting under the blankets. "Hopefully, Jensen will remember to stop and buy me some clothes," he said, beckoning Patrick to the makeshift bed. "Come here and let me hold you."

Patrick stared down at the welts, scars, and bandages littering his body. "After everything you've been through, I don't know why you'd still want anything to do with me." He gestured to his skinny, damaged body. "Or this."

Fisher whipped off the covers, exposing his naked body. "In case you failed to notice, I'm not looking so hot right now either."

All Patrick could see was the huge soft cock nestled against Fisher's hip. "You look good to me."

Fisher rolled to his side and propped his head up on his hand. "I'm freezing my ass off. Are you joining me?"

Patrick had no idea what was wrong with him. He'd wanted Fisher since the first day, but having sex with the man felt very inappropriate at the moment. "Actually, I think I'd like a bath first."

Fisher's black eyebrows drew together. "Are you feeling okay?"

"Yeah." Patrick picked up Fisher's robe. "Mind if I use this?"

"It's not mine, so go ahead." Fisher covered himself but continued to watch Patrick closely. "We don't have to do anything if the idea makes you uncomfortable."

Patrick wanted to deny Fisher's suspicion but couldn't. "There's something about this place." He tied the sash on the black silk robe. "It feels wrong," he admitted.

Fisher sat up. "I thought you said you felt warm for the first time in years."

"I did. I do." Patrick looked around the room. He wasn't sure how to explain it. "I think this room belonged to a holy man."

"It's an abbey. I imagine the whole damn place was full of holy men."

Patrick shook his head. "This one's different." Feeling sick to his stomach, he backed toward the door. "I need a minute."

CHAPTER FIVE

A knock on the door woke Fisher. "Yeah," he hollered, reaching for Patrick. When his arms came up empty, he panicked. "Shit." He threw off the covers and got to his feet. "Patrick!" he screamed, his heart racing.

The door opened and Jensen ran into the room. "He's in the sanctuary. Brian's with him, but he needs your help."

Fisher's chest tightened. Why the hell had he let himself fall asleep? The plan had been to give Patrick some time alone, but he'd never meant to fucking fall asleep. "Shit!" He searched the floor for something to put on until he realized the only thing he'd had to wear was the robe that Patrick had worn to the bathroom. "Let's go."

Jensen shot out of the room with Fisher on his heels. They ran down the long hallway through the kitchen and out the door. Fisher sped by Jensen and got to the church first. He threw open the door and came to a screeching halt. "Fuck me," he whispered at the scene in front of him. He hurried down the long, center aisle, wondering why Brian was just standing there instead of helping Patrick.

"Beautiful, isn't it?" Brian asked.

"What the hell's going on?" Fisher clenched his hands into fists. He'd take on anything or anyone to protect Patrick.

"I have no idea, but I'll find out," Brian replied. "He's obviously possessed, but how and by whom, I'm not sure."

Fisher knelt beside the prone naked body. "Patrick?"

Positioned in front of the altar, Patrick was lying on his stomach with his legs together and his arms stretched out to the side. *Damn.* Patrick resembled an alabaster cross. Fisher couldn't decide whether the glow that seemed to emanate from Patrick was coming from the beam of sunlight pouring over his thin body or from within.

Fisher picked up the discarded robe. He was tempted to put it on to shield his naked body from the others, but if Patrick had been lying on the cold stone floor all night, his body temperature had to be critically low.

"Patrick."

Patrick didn't acknowledge him, just continued to chant in…was it Latin? He waved, getting Brian's attention. "Is he speaking Latin?"

Brian nodded. "The same phrase over and over. Psalm ninety-one, one through sixteen."

"Which is?" Fisher asked. He wasn't as knowledgeable of Bible verses as Brian was.

"He who dwells in the shelter of the Most High will abide in the shadow of the Almighty. I will say to the Lord, "My refuge and my fortress, my God, in whom I trust." For he will deliver you from the snare of the fowler and from the deadly pestilence. He will cover you with his pinions, and under his wings you will find refuge; his faithfulness is a shield and buckler. You will not fear the terror of the night, nor the arrow that flies by day." Brian glanced from Fisher to Patrick. "I think whatever

allowed that spirit to possess him yesterday, is allowing a different one in today." He pointed to Patrick. "Only this one is trying to keep him safe."

"I've got to get him off this floor and warmed up," Fisher said. "Will this…spirit hurt him if I try to move him?"

Brian continued to stare at Patrick. "He has a lot of scars."

"Yeah." Fisher didn't like the way Brian was staring at Patrick's naked body. "Do you mind?" He covered Patrick with the robe.

Brian rolled his eyes. "He's not my type." He knelt down beside Patrick and ran his hand across the scars. "I need to check all of these. According to my grandfather's journal, spirits need an access point unless they're invited in, and since I don't think Patrick's welcomed his visitors, I'd say he has one."

"I'll look for it," Fisher said, trying to elbow Brian away from Patrick.

"Don't be stupid. You have no idea what you're looking for. Why don't you go get Patrick some blankets? Even if the spirit leaves Patrick's body, I think it'd be a good idea to keep him in the church."

"For how long?" Fisher asked. He looked around. Gavin and Jensen were forty yards away, still standing just inside the church. "There's nothing in here. How long do you expect him to stay?"

"Until I figure out what we're dealing with and how to stop it." Brian reached for Fisher's hand. "I came here to help. Let me do that. In the meantime, ask Gavin to get me everything he can about this church."

Fisher wasn't sure if it was important, but he remembered what Patrick said about the room they'd chosen to sleep in.

"I think the bedroom where Jensen found me is safe, too. Patrick said he felt warm in there for the first time in years."

Brian nodded. "For now just get blankets."

"Jensen can get the damn blankets! I'm not leaving him." Fisher was twice Brian's size, and he'd be damned if he'd be ordered into leaving.

Patrick screamed, cutting off any further protest from Fisher.

Fisher knocked Brian out of the way and lifted Patrick into his arms. The moment he had Patrick cradled in his arms, Patrick opened his eyes.

"Hurts," Patrick moaned.

"Where, baby?" Fisher stared down into Patrick's big blue eyes. "Tell me where it hurts."

Patrick reached up and touched his temple. "My head."

Fisher glanced at Brian. "Can I take him to our room?"

Brian shrugged. "I don't know." He tucked the robe around Patrick. "Your call."

Fisher closed his eyes and rested his forehead against Patrick's. He'd hold Patrick in his arms forever if only it was enough to protect him.

"Take me back to the room," Patrick said, breaking into Fisher's thoughts.

"Okay." With Patrick still in his arms, he got to his feet. The only thing he felt sure of was making Patrick as comfortable as he possibly could. Hell, he'd already proven that he couldn't protect him.

As Fisher carried Patrick out of the church, he made a promise to himself and whatever spirits were lurking. He'd never again take a moment of time with Patrick for granted.

* * * *

Patrick woke in Fisher's arms. "What time is it?"

Fisher picked up his phone. "Almost five." He pulled Patrick closer. "You hungry? Ian made lamb stew."

"Maybe later." Patrick kissed Fisher's chest. He needed details on what he'd done. The time lapse and waking up in the church were signs that he'd, once again, been *visited*. "Did I hurt you?"

Fisher stilled. "No. You didn't hurt anyone."

Patrick stared up at Fisher. "Then what did I do?" The visits were never good and often left behind a trail of destruction in one form or another.

"You prayed in Latin." Fisher scooted down on the pallet until they were eye to eye. "Evidently, one of the heavenly spirits who reside here decided to take a ride in your body. You...he...whoever, said you were safe as long as you're here. We know it's not a solution, but we're going to use the time here to figure out how to vanquish that sonofabitch."

"Did your friends get here?" Patrick vaguely remembered seeing another face when he'd been carried from the church.

"Yeah, Brian's the expert on paranormal shit, and Jensen's the man who protects him from the paranormal shit." Fisher grinned. "Like I want to protect you."

Patrick swallowed around the lump in his throat. Fisher had done more for him than anyone ever had. At first he'd questioned his growing feelings, wondering if they had something to do with Fisher's willingness to help him. The conclusion he'd come to was, hell yes, it had something to do with it. Fisher's belief in him since the beginning hadn't waivered. Combine Fisher's loyalty with his sweet disposition, caring touch, and killer body, and what else could a man possibly ask for?

"I know you're not going to believe me when I say this, but I need to say it anyway."

"I'll always believe you," Fisher said before Patrick could continue.

"I know." Patrick moved to straddle Fisher's groin, putting Fisher's cock against his ass. "That's why I think I'm falling in love with you."

Fisher shook his head but didn't push Patrick away. "You can't be in love with me."

Patrick felt the way Fisher's body had responded to the declaration. Despite what Fisher said, Patrick knew he liked hearing it. "I am, and there's nothing you can do about it."

"You're just grateful," Fisher protested, reaching for the bottle of lube.

"Put whatever label you want on it if that makes you feel better, but I know what I feel." Patrick took the lube from Fisher and squirted a good amount into his hand before moving back far enough to expose Fisher's cock. "Is this right?" he asked, spreading the lube up and down Fisher's length.

"Yeah," Fisher replied, his voice cracking. "Although you should also put some on your hole, too."

Patrick released Fisher's cock and reached back. He'd never applied lube before and found the sensation of his finger sliding around his hole pleasant. "Feels good," he said.

Fisher slicked his fingers. "Yeah? Just wait."

Patrick's breath caught when he felt Fisher touch his hole. "Oh," he groaned when Fisher pushed a finger inside. He wanted more. For years, he'd endured sex with only hate and pain involved. It made the contact with Fisher even more special because he knew any forthcoming pain would be welcome and most likely begged for, not that he planned to ask to be hurt, but he was a realist. There was a big difference between having a spirit's cock up his ass and having Fisher's big meat fucking him.

Confident that any pain would be worth it, Patrick climbed off Fisher, dislodging Fisher's finger. He lay on his back and spread his legs. "This is the way people make love, right?"

Fisher sat up. "It's the people involved, not the position." He moved between Patrick's spread thighs. "I'm too heavy to lay on top of you, but I'll make it work."

"Thank you," Patrick whispered.

"Drape your legs over my shoulders," Fisher instructed, smearing more lube on Patrick's hole.

The position left Patrick feeling vulnerable. *Exposed.* He took a deep breath and tried to remember that Fisher would never hurt him.

Fisher pressed the head of his cock against Patrick's hole. "You sure you don't want me to stretch you some more?"

"I'm sure." Patrick wanted to feel Fisher before the room began to swallow him again. He still wasn't sure who the spirit was that resided in the bedroom, but he felt the presence hovering nearby.

Fisher pushed the tip of his cock inside Patrick before stopping. He stared down at Patrick. "Tell me when I can go farther."

Patrick smiled up at Fisher. "It doesn't hurt." He chuckled. "I thought it would, but it doesn't." Whether it was the protective spirit or the fact that he'd lived with pain for so long that his threshold was high, he didn't know, but he needed more. He needed everything Fisher had to give.

Fisher's jaw ticked several times as he pushed inside. "So fucking tight."

The comment made Patrick feel good. He might be wrong, but it sounded like Fisher liked the way he felt, and if he liked it, maybe Fisher would want to do it again.

"What should I do?"

Fisher didn't say anything until his cock was fully seated in Patrick's ass. "Just tell me when I can move."

Patrick could see the tension in Fisher's arms and neck. He reached up and touched Fisher's face. "Are you mad at me?"

Fisher blinked. "What?" he ground out between clenched teeth.

"You look like you're mad," Patrick replied.

"Being inside of you is better than anything I've ever felt. I'm having a little trouble controlling myself, but I will. You don't have to worry."

"I'm fine. You don't have to control yourself," Patrick argued. He wanted everything Fisher was willing to give him.

"No. This is about making love. I wanna prove to you that sex doesn't have to hurt," Fisher explained, easing his cock out of Patrick.

"But I thought you said making love was about the people involved?" Patrick grabbed Fisher's hips and tried to pull him back, wanting the feel of Fisher's cock inside of him again. "I think if I like it and you like it, that's all that should matter."

Fisher followed Patrick's lead and slid back inside. He closed his eyes and shook his head. "I need to fuck you hard. I can't explain this uncontrollable need because it doesn't make sense, even to me, but that's what I need to do."

Patrick thought about it for a few seconds. Fisher had given him comfort and kindness when everyone else had shut him out. He'd also told Patrick that he wanted to make love to him. With his mind made up, Patrick pushed against Fisher's chest.

"Give me a second."

Fisher opened his eyes and backed off. "What's wrong?"

Patrick rolled over. "Nothing. I just decided we should do it this way." He got to his knees, shoving his ass into the air, and rested his cheek on the pillow.

Fisher's cock entered Patrick from behind. He sighed as he buried his cock as deep as it would go. "You feel so good."

Patrick sighed with each thrust. When he was in his early teens, he had fantasized about having sex.

Fisher draped himself over Patrick's back and whispered in his ear. "I'm falling in love with you."

Although Patrick felt the same way, he couldn't understand why a man like Fisher would fall for someone like him. "Why?" he finally asked. "You could have anyone."

Fisher continued to pump in and out of him when he spoke. "I've had a lot of men, but none of them were you."

Patrick turned his head to meet Fisher's gaze. He tried to figure out what Fisher meant by that but decided to let it go because he knew that every moment with him was precious. If he let himself, he knew he could get lost in dreaming of a future where he could live with Fisher like a normal person, but the truth was, the attacks were coming more frequently. Most likely, he had a matter of days before his fate was sealed. The important thing was to keep Fisher and the others safe. So, yes, he needed to hold each precious moment close. With that in mind, he pushed all worries to the wayside and gave himself fully to the overwhelming pleasure of Fisher's cock inside him.

"How do you like to be jacked?" Fisher asked as he pumped and squeezed Patrick's erection.

Patrick's body went rigid at the sensations coursing through his body. "By your hand evidently," he managed to say just before coming. He was slightly embarrassed that he'd climaxed so quickly, but he had a feeling most men would have done the same if they were in his place. His heart thumped at the idea of someone else making love with Fisher.

"Fuck, babe," Fisher growled as he began to rub the ejaculate across the skin of Patrick's stomach. "Never had a man hotter than you." He thrust several more times before crying out. "Mine."

Patrick wrapped the word around him as he sank onto the pallet of blankets with Fisher still on top of him. He almost protested when Fisher pulled out of him, but smiled instead when a soft kiss landed on his shoulder.

"I'll get something to clean us up," Fisher whispered in Patrick's ear.

Patrick nodded. He wasn't sure what he loved most about Fisher, the fact that he always took care of him or how he fucked. He grinned as he admitted to himself that he wanted more of the latter before his time was up.

* * * *

Pulling on the clothes Ian had loaned him, Patrick left Fisher sleeping and went in search of Brian. When he passed Sal's room, he stopped to check on him, but was surprised to find the bed empty. He found Brian, Jensen, and Ian huddled around the kitchen table. The three men stopped talking the moment Patrick entered the room.

"How're you feeling?" Brian asked. He got to his feet and held out his hand. "I'm Brian, by the way. We didn't get a chance to formally meet earlier." He gestured to the handsome man at his side. "This is Jensen."

"Nice to meet you." Patrick shook hands with the men he recognized from the pictures on Fisher's living room wall. "Where's Sal?"

Ian's shoulders drooped in a defeated posture. "He's in the church talking to Gavin about what happened. The two of them have always been pretty close."

Patrick nodded. He'd noticed the way Gavin's gaze seemed to track Sal's every move. If he wasn't mistaken, Ian had noticed it as well. His heart went out to Ian, but it wasn't really his place to get involved in their domestic situation.

He turned his attention to the stack of old books in the center of the table. "Did you find anything?"

Brian adjusted his glasses. "Maybe, but I'd like to discuss the situation with everyone at the same time. Would you mind getting Gavin and Sal while I talk to Fisher for a minute?"

Patrick wondered why Brian wanted to speak with Fisher alone but didn't push. "Sure."

Patrick made his way out of the abbey. He tipped his head back in an effort to determine the time of day. The sun wasn't directly overhead, but not far off. Satisfied, he continued to the church. He was outside the open door when he overheard Sal and Gavin talking.

"Stop it," Sal ordered, his voice leaving no doubt he was getting angry.

"Come on," Gavin whined. "We used to fuck all the time."

"That was before Ian," Sal returned. "You've got a good thing going with him. Don't screw it up."

"Ian's cheap labor. Other than that, we fuck and nothing more."

Patrick rubbed his chest at the cold words. He couldn't believe Gavin would talk about Ian like that. Worse, he knew Ian had real feelings for Gavin.

He cleared his throat. "Brian wants us in the kitchen," he said before turning back toward the abbey.

* * * *

Fisher opened his eyes to find Brian sitting on the blanket beside him. He immediately sat straight up. "Where's Patrick?"

"He went to the church to get Gavin and Sal. I wanted a minute to talk to you before we join the others." Brian handed Fisher a pair of new jeans. "Do me a favor and cover up your junk before Jensen comes in and has a stroke."

Fisher grinned when he realized he was not only naked but the blanket had been kicked off at some point during sleep. He tore the tag off the jeans before getting to his feet.

"Jesus!" Brian quickly looked away while Fisher pulled his pants on. "We bought other stuff for you and Patrick, but these are all I grabbed on my way in. I'm not sure how much time we'll have before someone bursts in on us, and it's important."

"So talk." Fisher zipped the jeans and was surprised to find that his usual size now hung a little loose on his hips.

"After what happened in the church, I walked nearly every inch of the property. I can't be positive, but it seems the grounds are protected. I found menhirs erected around the perimeter with Christian Horns, facing outward, chiseled into them."

Fisher shook his head. "You've already lost me. What's a menhir?"

"A standing stone. I'll show them to you later. The important thing is, I've never seen them arranged like that around a church, so I started digging, and I discovered something very interesting in one of the books Gavin found when he started renovating the abbey—a journal that belonged to one of the monks. First of all, the abbey and church were built by an order called the Cistercian Order. They followed the teachings of Saint Bernard, who believed in manual labor and self-sufficiency. In other words, they were farmers who lived a simple life that they believed brought them closer to God. The journal had a lot of entries about crop yield and daily life accounting, which leads me to believe the monk who kept it was the order's bookkeeper, but he documented incidents as well."

Fisher fought to keep his impatience at bay. "Okay. Do these incidents have anything to do with what's going on with Patrick?"

"I think so, although I don't know if they involve the same spirits who are attacking Patrick. According to the book, the order learned of a group of men and women in the nearby town who practiced satanic worship along with witchcraft. It's hard to say whether or not the group really was doing such a thing, but the monks and other townspeople believed it. There were rumors of sacrifices, orgies, cannibalism, and…" Brian paused and met Fisher's gaze, "—possession rituals."

Fisher's breath hitched. "And?" he prompted.

"The menhirs scattered like sentries around the property's boundaries tell me the monks were trying to keep the evil out of their sanctuary. Unfortunately, the safety only lasted while the monks were on the grounds because over a twenty-three-year period, thirty-four monks were either killed or committed suicide. The last straw for the order was finding thirteen of their brothers hanging from a large oak tree a hundred yards from the property line. The journal has a few drawings that depict images they found carved into the tree before the surviving monks burned it to the ground."

Fisher remembered seeing a large patch of bare earth beside the road leading to the church and knew in his gut that's where the tree once stood. "Do you recognize any of them?"

Brian nodded. "They're basic satanic symbols." He got to his feet. "I told you this morning that I needed to check Patrick's body for an entry point, and that hasn't changed."

At the moment, Fisher wished he knew as much about spirits as Brian because the last thing he wanted was another man searching every inch of the man he'd fallen in love with.

"I'm not sure why you can't just tell me what you're looking for, and let me do it."

"Because I don't really know what it'll look like. It all depends on how the mark got there. If a ritual was performed, the wound could be a specific cut or burn. I've even heard of an entire lineage being cursed. In those cases, there's a birthmark that is passed down through the generations."

"That's probably it," Fisher said. "Patrick said his dad went crazy before he died, and from the sound of it, so did his grandpa."

"Hey, is Patrick in here with you?" Sal asked, opening the door.

Fisher tensed. "I thought he went to find you?" He started toward Sal, gently pushing his friend out of the way.

"He did, but when Gavin and I got to the kitchen, Jensen said he hadn't come back," Sal said, following Fisher down the hall. "Ian went out to look for him, and Jensen and Gavin are searching the rest of the abbey."

Fisher took off at a run, flying through the kitchen on his way outside. "Patrick!" he called, scanning the area.

"Down there," Brian said, pointing toward the bottom of the hill.

Fisher felt like his heart would pound out of his chest when he realized what was happening. "Patrick!" he yelled as loud as he could as he rushed down the slope.

On the protected side of the menhirs, Patrick didn't turn or acknowledge Fisher, but continued to watch as Ian's lean body was continually tossed through the air.

"Fuck!" Brian swore as he flew by Fisher with a youthful speed Fisher no longer had in him.

Before Fisher could reach Patrick, Ian let out a bone-chilling scream.

Ian's slender body landed hard approximately fifteen yards from Patrick, bleeding heavily through his thin, worn T-shirt. Thankfully, he curled himself into a ball in an attempt to protect himself.

Patrick simply stared without an ounce of visible emotion.

Fisher wasn't sure how the possessing spirit that had taken over Patrick would react to his touch, but he had no choice. Allowing Patrick to step beyond the protective border wasn't an option.

He wrapped his arm around Patrick's waist and spoke into his ear. "I don't know who you are, but I need you to take Patrick back to the abbey and wait for me there."

Patrick tilted his head back and stared up at Fisher with a blank gaze before pointing toward Ian. "Vanquish lui."

Fisher looked over at Jensen who had appeared out of nowhere and was currently struggling with Brian, who obviously wanted to help poor Ian. "What'd he say?"

"Vanquish him," Gavin replied.

Fisher whipped his head around, surprised to find Gavin a few feet away. "Why're you just standing there?"

Gavin gestured toward Ian. "He's a black belt. If he can't handle himself, there's not a lot I can do to stop whatever the fuck's going on."

Moving slowly, Sal pushed Gavin out of the way. "You sorry sonofabitch," he growled as he neared the property line.

"Are you nuts," Gavin said. "Do you really think you're healthy enough to go up against that ghost again?"

Sal's black eyebrows rose. "Guess we'll find out."

Struggling against Jensen's hold, Brian warned, "Be careful. Get in, grab Ian, then get the fuck back here."

Fisher warred with himself as he watched Sal cross the boundary. Gavin had been right, Sal wasn't physically well enough to go a round with the evil spirit.

He physically turned Patrick toward the abbey. "Please, take the man I love back to safety."

Without blinking, Patrick started back up the long slope, repeating his earlier phrase as he went. Satisfied that Patrick was out of danger, Fisher spun around and charged into the fray. Immediately, he was hit from the side and nearly lost his footing, but he managed to right himself as he took another step toward Ian who was still under attack. *Fuck. How many were there?*

With his earlier stitched wound reopened, Sal sank to the ground beside Ian and did his best to protect the much smaller man with his own body, but it wasn't enough. Ian let out another cry from under Sal just as Fisher's legs were knocked out from under him. A burning sensation worked its way down Fisher's calf as Fisher kicked out.

Jensen's arms wrapped around Fisher's upper torso. "Come on, buddy, let's get you outta here." He began to drag him across the grass toward the warded property.

"Don't worry about me," Fisher argued. "Help Sal with Ian. I don't think either of them can take much more."

"Shit!" Jensen released Fisher. "Brian, go to the abbey and check on Patrick."

Unable to stand, Fisher used his forearms to snake across the ground toward safety. He spotted Jensen carrying an unconscious Ian out of the corner of his eye and prayed the two would make it to the property in time.

"Sal," he called.

"Yeah," Sal returned. "I'm good, just go."

Before Fisher could cross fully between the upright stone wards, another deep gash scored across his back. "Fuck!" he howled in pain.

Gavin finally decided to stop being a pussy and grabbed Fisher by the wrists, pulling him to the holy grounds.

Two seconds after being released, Fisher turned back and reached for Sal's hand, doing the same favor for him.

Sal struggled to his feet and tore Ian out of Jensen's hold. "Give him to me."

Jensen shook his head. "What the fuck just happened?"

Fisher let Jensen help him up but leaned heavily against his friend. "There had to be at least three of them. I don't understand why they're so drawn to this place."

Supporting Fisher, Jensen followed Sal up the hill. "I'm hoping whoever's protecting Patrick can give us some answers."

CHAPTER SIX

Wiping tears from his face, Patrick did his best to concentrate on closing the last of Ian's lacerations. They'd run out of thread, which he'd used to sew up Sal's wounds, so he'd been forced to use Super Glue on Fisher's leg, Jensen's back and arms, and poor Ian's entire body.

"I can't do this anymore," he mumbled with a hitch in his breath.

"Shhh." Fisher stepped close enough to land a kiss on Patrick's temple. "We're all going to be fine."

Patrick jerked his head away from Fisher's lips. The understanding emanating from everyone was getting on his nerves. Except for Brian and Gavin, everyone he'd come into contact with had put their lives on the line for him. Ian's pale and freckled skin would forever be marred by a roadmap of scars because of him.

He used his forearm to wipe away the tears again before tying off the last stitch. "Will you watch him?"

Sal, who was lying next to Ian, nodded. "Like a hawk." He brushed his thumb down Ian's cheek.

Patrick wasn't sure what was going on with the pair but decided it wasn't his business. He moved away from the bed to rinse his bloody hands in the pail of warm water Gavin had set out.

"I want to talk to Brian."

"He's still in with Jensen," Fisher replied.

"Would you please ask him to meet me in the church when he can?" Patrick asked as he walked out of the room.

"Wait," Fisher called. "I don't want you going to the church alone. Just give me a second, and I'll talk to Brian before I come with you."

Patrick scraped his teeth over his bottom lip several times. "I want to talk to Brian alone, but you can sit with me until he comes. Okay?"

"Wait right there." Fisher limped toward the room Brian and Jensen were using while Patrick leaned against the wall.

"Patrick," Sal called.

Worried that Ian had started to bleed again, Patrick rushed back to the room. "Is he okay?"

Sal smiled down at Ian before returning his attention to Patrick. "He'll be fine. I just wanted to thank you for spending the last three hours taking care of us."

Guilt settled like a stone in Patrick's gut. "If it weren't for me, none of you would've been hurt in the first place."

Sal's dark brown eyes narrowed. "None of this is your fault. You didn't ask for it, and you didn't do anything to deserve it. Evidently, the spirits were already here. Talk to Gavin if you don't believe me. There've been unexplained murders in this area for several hundred years. I have a feeling you hold the key that'll lock these evil bastards in hell forever."

* * * *

Fisher sat in one of the covered church pews with his arm wrapped tightly around Patrick. He didn't like the idea of Patrick talking to Brian alone because it meant Patrick wanted to keep something from him. Hell, he wouldn't put it past Patrick to offer himself up as a sacrifice if it meant saving everyone else. No way would he let that happen.

"I love you," he whispered.

"I love you, too." Patrick ran his fingertips down Fisher's stubbled jaw. "But you have to know I can't go on like this. I don't know what can be done, but I'm willing to try anything to make this stop. I'm hoping Brian has answers, but if he doesn't…" He sighed. "I'd rather die trying than live like this."

Fisher started to argue, but Patrick covered his mouth with his hand.

"If the situation was reversed, you'd do the same thing, and don't tell me you wouldn't. You keep putting yourself between me and those trying to harm me, and I can't let you do that anymore."

Fisher gently pulled Patrick's hand away. He'd heard enough. "Then we'll do it together, because now that I have you, I can't imagine living without you."

A noise from the doorway drew Fisher's attention. He looked up and spotted Brian across the large open sanctuary. "Let me stay while you talk to Brian. Please?" He'd never begged for anything in his life, but he'd get on his hands and knees if that's what it took to convince Patrick.

"You have to promise me that if Brian has an idea on how to stop this, you'll let me do it," Patrick warned him.

Fisher had worked with Brian and Jensen to rid Alcatraz of its ghosts, so he knew how dangerous things could get, but he understood where Patrick was coming from. He could've walked away from Alcatraz before the shit rained down on them, but he'd chosen to stay and fight beside his friends.

"As long as you'll let me stand by you." He bent down for a deep kiss, giving himself time to explore Patrick's mouth before pulling back. "You ready to talk to Brian?"

Patrick nodded.

Fisher lifted his arm and waved Brian over, noticing the worried expression on Brian's face. For someone who'd made a career of dealing with evil spirits, the fact that Brian was uneasy told Fisher more than words could. Whatever they were up against, it wouldn't be easy to vanquish.

Carrying the ledger he'd found in the abbey, Brian sat beside Patrick.

"How's Jensen?" Patrick asked.

Brian reached for Patrick's hand. "He's good. Resting."

Fisher noticed Patrick eyeing the leather-bound book. "Do you know what that is?" He half expected the monk to jump into Patrick's body at any second.

Patrick started to reach for the book but pulled back before making contact. "It doesn't look familiar, but I'm drawn to it." His gaze went to Brian. "What is it?"

Brian opened the journal. "This was written by the spirit I believe has entered you at least twice. It's your typical ledger in the beginning, but toward the back—" He flipped pages. "—it goes into more detail about life at the abbey. Well, actually, it goes into detail about the deaths of quite a few of the monks who resided here. There's a brief passage about twelve monks and one priest who were found hanging from a tree outside the protected grounds." He sighed and tapped the last written page. "Unfortunately, it doesn't go into detail, which is odd because it's also the final entry."

"Okay," Patrick replied.

Brian leaned closer to Patrick. "I need to know more about the deaths of those monks if I'm going to figure out how to battle the evil outside the property."

"Okay," Patrick repeated. "How can I help?"

Brian met Fisher's gaze over Patrick's head. "I need to talk to the monk who possessed you."

Fisher wrapped his arm tighter around Patrick. He'd had a feeling that would be Brian's suggestion, but because the spirit had entered Patrick before without harming him, he didn't protest.

"I don't have any control over that." Patrick fidgeted. "I'd do it if I could, though."

Brian held out the book. "Hold this for me." He glanced at Fisher. "You might want to release him and scoot down on the bench."

Still feeling uneasy about the whole thing, Fisher tilted Patrick's chin around to look into his eyes. "I'll be here for you," he whispered against Patrick's lips before claiming them in a deep kiss. Breaking for air, he rested his forehead against Patrick's. "Remember when I told you I'd never let anything harm you?"

Patrick nodded.

Fisher kissed him again. "I meant it."

Patrick licked his lips. "Think of some things we can do after this is over."

"What kind of things?" Fisher asked.

"Normal things. I don't really know what couples do when they aren't fighting off ghosts or running for their lives." Patrick's face lit up. "Except that big round bed-thing you have on your deck. I know I want to curl up in that with you. Maybe we could eat McDonald's again. I'd like that a lot."

Christ. Fisher's heart melted. He couldn't wait to show Patrick all that life had to offer, but there was no way in hell he'd take Patrick back to the town whose people had turned their backs on him.

"We can do that, and a whole lot more."

"Thanks. I'd like that." Patrick pushed against Fisher's chest. "Let me do this, so we can get to that other stuff."

"Right." Fisher hesitated for only a moment before releasing Patrick. He moved to the end of the old pew.

Patrick turned back to Brian. "I'm ready."

Brian lifted the ledger once again before holding it out to Patrick. "Hold this against you, and try your best to clear your mind."

The moment the book was in his hands, Patrick's entire body jerked twice and a stream of French poured from his lips.

"Shit. I was afraid of that. My French is rusty at best. I'd hoped it would be Latin again." Brian looked at Fisher. "Go get Gavin."

Fisher hated to leave Patrick, but the point of allowing the spirit in was gathering information, which they couldn't do without Gavin. He shot out of the pew as fast as his injured leg would allow and didn't stop until he found Gavin in the abbey's kitchen.

"We need you in the church."

Gavin finished his drink. "Find someone else. I'm done with that shit."

Anger filled Fisher. "We just need you to translate, you fucking coward. The threat is out there, not in here." He didn't wait for Gavin to answer before grabbing him by the back of the neck. "Now, either you come with me on your own, or I'll throw you over my shoulder and carry you to the church."

Gavin tried to knock Fisher's hand away, but Fisher was having none of it.

"Fine!" Gavin shouted before standing. "But you'd better figure it out quick and get your freak off my property before those ghosts come back."

Fisher shoved Gavin toward the door. "You don't get it, do you? Those ghosts have always been here. Patrick's presence has simply fueled the rage between whatever evil's on the outside of your land and the good that's on the inside. Patrick's nothing more than a vessel in this fight."

Gavin stalked his way to the church while muttering curse words under his breath.

Fisher pushed open the heavily-carved double doors and gestured for Gavin to enter. "Go sit behind Patrick and see if you can figure out what he's saying."

Gavin scowled at Fisher but didn't protest the order.

"He's been talking nonstop since you left," Brian said as Fisher resumed his seat at the end of the pew. "I followed him in the beginning, but he's too fast for me." He tapped Patrick's arm and pointed over his shoulder to Gavin. "Tell him," he said in French.

Patrick stood and turned to face Gavin before launching into fluent French. Gavin's eyes went wide. "He says the children in the village began to disappear first, then women were taken, impregnated, and returned." Gavin held up his hand and shook his head.

Patrick stopped speaking.

"The villagers came to the abbey begging for help, but the abbot at the time wouldn't allow the monks to leave the church grounds because he claimed God couldn't protect them," Gavin relayed before signaling for Patrick to continue.

Patrick's hand slashed through the air as his tone turned angry.

"When pregnant women were found with their stomachs cut open and their infants missing, the monks could no longer turn away the grieving villagers. A group of monks left the safety of the grounds and traveled to a series of caves where the villagers claimed rituals were taking place."

Gavin gestured to Patrick. "The abbot was away, and Brother Callum had been left in charge, so he stayed behind. He doesn't know how his brothers were able to do it, but the high priest of the satanic sect along with three others were killed by the monks. In an effort to hide what they'd done, the monks buried the bodies under the ancient oak at the bottom of the hill."

Gavin fisted his hands in his hair and shook his head as if he could shut Patrick's words out. "The next morning, Brother Callum discovered thirteen of his fellow monks hanging from the tree. Callum couldn't decipher the symbols carved into the tree, but the survivors all felt the evil when they cut their brothers down and carried them back to the abbey. They buried their dead and burned the tree, hoping that would be the end of it, but a week later, the abbot was killed in a freak accident just outside the grounds."

Gavin, once again, gestured to Patrick. "Brother Callum and the surviving monks never left the safety of the property again. One by one, the monks died of sickness or old age until only Brother Callum remained."

Patrick started to cry and sank onto the pew. "Brother Callum did his best to bury his brothers, but by the end, the loneliness and guilt drove him to end his own life."

"That's why Callum is still here," Brian whispered to Fisher.

Fisher nodded in agreement.

Brian grabbed Gavin's arm. "Ask him if he'll help us get rid of the evil surrounding the church when the time comes. Then ask him to release Patrick until we need him again."

Gavin huffed before relaying Brian's message.

Fisher started to slide down the pew toward Patrick, needing his man in his arms in the worst way.

"*Oui*," Patrick said a moment before he began to slump to the floor.

Fisher moved fast and caught Patrick in his arms. He sank onto the pew, cradling Patrick even closer against his chest, and thanked God he'd made the decision to check on Patrick that day back in Hickory County.

"Am I done now?" Gavin looked annoyed, and it took all Fisher's strength not to take the man down.

"For now," Brian replied as he retrieved the ledger from the floor. "We need to decide how we're going to proceed."

"Give me and Patrick an hour or so for him to recover," Fisher said, making no move to leave with Brian and Gavin.

"Sure," Brian replied.

Fisher ran his free hand over Patrick's closely-cropped black hair. "You feel okay?"

"Groggy, but I'm okay." Patrick ran his fingertips over Fisher's jaw. "You still haven't shaved."

Fisher grinned. "Shaving's been the last thing on my mind, although, I need to kiss you. You mind a little whisker burn?"

Patrick's lips parted in silent need before he shook his head.

Fisher rearranged Patrick to straddle his lap. If it were any other time and they weren't sitting in a church, he might've tried to take things further than a simple kiss, but with luck, there would be years to explore all the wonders Patrick's body had to offer. Their location didn't stop them from indulging in several very heated, very deep kisses, however.

"That was nice," Patrick said.

"Yeah," Fisher agreed. "I've been giving some thought to what I want to do with you when all this is behind us."

"And?"

"And, I want us to get the hell out of Hickory County. If you could move anywhere in the world, where would it be?" Fisher asked.

"I don't know. I've never been anywhere other than here, and I'm not sure I like it here," Patrick confessed.

"Understandable." For years, Fisher had longed for a real home, but he'd realized over the past week that it wasn't a home at all that he'd wanted. It was someone who made life worth living again. "Maybe the two of us could do some traveling. I'd love to introduce you to the beaches of the Caribbean and the mountains of Switzerland."

"If I could stay with you, I'd settle for a cabin by a lake in Colorado." Patrick smiled at Fisher for one brilliant moment before his expression turned troubled. "My father will eventually find me, though, so maybe it would be better if we just went back."

"Why would you say that?" Fisher couldn't believe Patrick would willingly go back to the hell he'd lived before.

"Because I don't want to fall deeper in love with you knowing what's out there waiting to take everything away. There were times when I could feel my father in the room, but he wouldn't touch me. I'd wait for the blow to come for hours, and I think that was even more torture than being hit. Finally, I'd have enough and start saying things to provoke him just to get it over with." Patrick cupped Fisher's face in his hands. "I can't live in heaven while waiting for hell."

Fisher closed his eyes. There had to be a way to keep Patrick's father away from him. He opened his eyes when he remembered what Brian had said about searching Patrick's body.

"Do you have a birthmark?"

Patrick tilted his head to the side. "Huh?"

"A birthmark. Do you have one?" Fisher asked again.

Patrick nodded. "On the bottom of my foot."

Fisher lifted Patrick off his lap and set him on the pew. "Let me see it. Which foot is it on?"

Patrick rested his right ankle on his left knee before pulling off his shoe and sock. "When I was young, I wished it was somewhere people could see it. You know, like a tattoo because my father had it, too, and I thought that was pretty cool."

Fisher bent over and examined the faint reddish-brown mark on Patrick's instep. It was a perfect triangle with Celtic symbol in the center, so clean it could have been inked into Patrick's skin.

"You say your father had one, too?"

"Yeah. He said it was a gift from our ancestors."

Fisher gestured to Patrick's sock and shoe. "Put those back on, and let's go find Brian."

* * * *

Fisher leaned against the doorway as Brian poured over several old books that had once belonged to his grandfather.

"Anything?" Fisher asked.

Brian glanced up before returning his attention to the book in his lap. "Well, I know what the symbol means. Evidently, someone in Patrick's family tree agreed to be marked and sacrificed at the hand of someone very powerful in satanic worship." He tapped the drawing beside him of the mark on Patrick's heel. "The triangle is a portal of sorts. The symbol inside it is a simple initial, but the filigree around it, suggests power and wealth."

With a dramatic sigh, Brian closed the book before reaching for another. "The birthmark leaves Patrick completely open to the evil that we both know roams the world. It also makes him vulnerable to possession."

A rush of emotion threatened to overwhelm Fisher. He was glad Patrick was down the hall checking on Ian and Sal because he was supposed to be the strong one in their relationship. He'd built his life around being the man people leaned on and went to for help. What would Patrick think of him if he saw the tears brimming in his eyes?

"Is there anything we can do?"

"Completely?" Brian shook his head. "I don't think so. I'm assuming the mark goes deep into the tissue of his foot. Short of amputation, there's probably no way to completely excise it."

Fisher bent over and picked up one of the books. He started flipping pages, searching for something—anything.

Brian cleared his throat as he gently took the book from Fisher's hands. "You won't find what you're looking for." He licked his lips. "I may not be able to rid Patrick of the portal, but I might be able to change it."

"Change it?" Fisher grabbed Brian's thin shoulders. "How?"

Brian held up his hands. "I don't even know if it'll work, and it isn't going to be pain-free, so it needs to be Patrick's decision."

"What do you mean?" Fisher felt like he'd almost won a race only to have someone trip him just before crossing the finish line.

"How's a man supposed to sleep with you two arguing," Jensen mumbled from his pallet.

Brian crawled to Jensen's side. "How're you feeling?"

"Like I've gone five rounds with a psycho." Jensen grinned. "Reminds me of old times."

Brian leaned down and kissed Jensen before pulling back. "Are you up for a plan?"

Jensen let out a groan as he struggled to sit up. He looked at the wounds on his arms. "The glue seems to be holding, so I guess so. How're Sal and Ian?"

"Sal's a tough sonofabitch, so he's already up and around, but Ian's going to take a while before he's back on his feet," Patrick said from behind Fisher.

Fisher turned and drew Patrick into his arms. "How long've you been back there?"

"Not long." Patrick slipped his arm around Fisher's waist. "Did you find anything in your books, Brian?"

Brian nodded. "I think so, but we can't really try anything anyway until we come up with a plan to dig up the bones the monks buried."

"Did I miss something?" Jensen asked.

* * * *

"This is all I have," Ian said, setting an expensive-looking bag of salt on the table. "It's my beloved Fleur de sel, so use it wisely."

Patrick picked up the canvas bag and looked at the French writing. "You buy special salt?"

Ian slowly lowered himself in a kitchen chair. Sal had made sure to put a pillow against the spindled back, but it still looked as though Ian was in a great deal of pain.

"The only reason you're asking is because you haven't tasted it."

Patrick watched as Sal adjusted Ian's pillow. He'd noticed the way Sal seemed to hover over Ian, and he was still confused as to what was going on between Sal, Ian, and Gavin. He looked over at Gavin who was sitting on a wooden bench by the door. Arms crossed over his chest, Gavin looked more bored than angry that his friend was taking care of the man who was supposed to be his boyfriend.

Jensen took the bag from Patrick and seemed to weigh it with his hand. "Is this going to be enough?" he asked Brian.

"It's going to have to be. There are only four skeletons, so we'll just have to use it wisely." Brian glanced at Gavin. "Did you find the watering cans?"

Gavin nodded. "Only have two of them, but I put them next to the pump."

"And the shovels?" Jensen asked.

"Two spades, one pick, and two scoop shovels. All out and ready to go," Gavin replied.

"I still don't understand how you're going to dig up the graves without getting attacked again." Patrick reached for Fisher's hand. He didn't like the plan at all because he wasn't sure he could handle someone getting hurt again.

"Because it's you they're attracted to. They'd love nothing more than to gain control of you. I'm sure you're even more appealing to them when Brother Callum possesses you since he's partially responsible for their deaths," Brian explained.

"I'll stay with Patrick to make sure he's safe," Gavin declared.

"The hell you will," Sal growled. "Ian's not physically well enough to help us dig or to fight off any ghosts that come calling. There's not a fucking scratch on you."

"And it's going to stay that way." Gavin set his jaw. Obviously, his mind was made up.

Patrick didn't really want anyone with him, but he'd agreed to have Ian accompany him because he knew Ian wanted to help and wouldn't survive another attack.

Sal stood so fast his chair tipped over. "You fucking pussy." With his hands curled into fists, he stalked toward Gavin.

Gavin's eyes narrowed as he sneered at Sal. "You've got a lot of nerve. You come into *my* house and try to steal Ian from me."

Fisher got to his feet and stepped between the two men. "That's enough."

Sal pointed straight at Gavin. "I didn't have to steal him from you. You've treated him like slave labor for over six years. All I've done is shown him how a real man is supposed to treat someone as wonderful as he is."

"Fuck you!" Gavin yelled.

Patrick tore his gaze away from the arguing men to glance at Ian. It wasn't hard to see how the exchange between Sal and Gavin was affecting him. Patrick moved to set right the chair Sal had been sitting in.

"Why don't we go back to your room so I can clean and apply fresh bandages to your wounds."

Ian rose without a word and walked out of the kitchen.

Patrick looked back to Fisher and gestured to Ian. Fisher gave him a chin dip. Satisfied, Patrick followed down the hall. He was surprised when Ian walked right by the only room with an actual bed and entered one of the vacant rooms several doors down. A pallet made of one thin blanket had been made in the center of the room.

"I don't think it's good for you to lie on the cold floor."

Ian shrugged. "The bed belongs to Gavin," he mumbled as he unbuttoned his olive green camp shirt.

"I'll be right back." Patrick jogged to the room he shared with Fisher. He retrieved the box of first aid supplies and the thickest of the blankets he'd been given when they'd arrived. Returning to Ian's new room, he handed over the small box. "Hold this." He picked up the thin blanket and replaced it with the thicker one. "Use the lighter one to cover up with."

"But that's your blanket," Ian said, gesturing to the new pallet.

"Fisher's like an oven. I won't get cold." Patrick pointed to the blanket. "Sit."

Ian sank to the floor.

Patrick dug out the bottle of peroxide and several cotton balls. The glued cuts looked great, but he figured they both needed a distraction. He dabbed at the longest wound on Ian's lean but sculpted chest.

"I'm sorry about these."

Ian glanced down at his chest before meeting Patrick's eyes. "They aren't your fault. I imagine you don't believe that, but it's the truth. I've felt something off about this place since the day I arrived. To be honest, I probably wouldn't have taken the job because of it, but Gavin was very charming in the beginning."

"In the beginning?" Patrick questioned.

"Yeah. The first few years were great, in my opinion, but the last three have been iffy. Gavin leaves for months at a time. He says he has to make money, which I understand. The restoration on this place isn't cheap, but he's different when he comes home. I've always suspected he was seeing other people, but I never knew for sure and he has always denied it."

"So why'd you stay?" Patrick wasn't sure what he'd do if Fisher wanted to have sex with someone else. He figured he'd probably let Fisher do whatever he needed to do as long as it meant he didn't leave him for good.

"Because I've put my heart and soul into this place. In a way, I think of it more as mine than Gavin's." Ian shrugged. "Besides, I don't have anywhere else to go. I put my savings into the restoration, and it takes all the money Gavin earns to keep the place going, so there isn't anything left over to pay me."

Patrick wasn't sure what to say. He didn't have experience in relationships, so he probably shouldn't offer advice, but he'd seen the way Sal looked at Ian. "What about Sal? Do you like him?"

The corner of Ian's lip quirked. "I used to try and keep myself busy when he came around to talk to Gavin. There's something about him that's always made me nervous. He's always watched me so closely that I thought he was jealous because I was with Gavin and he wanted Gavin, but after today, I'm starting to wonder."

Patrick had witnessed the care Sal took with Ian. "He's into you," he felt confident saying. "I don't know him very well, but he acts protective of you like Fisher does with me."

"Yeah, I noticed that, too, but it's not like I can go from one man to another in a day."

Patrick finished with the cuts on Ian's chest and arms and moved around to the back. "I haven't had a very good life, so maybe I'm just really messed up about this stuff, but I think you should do what makes you feel good. If Sal makes you feel good, why would you be without him?"

"Patrick?" Fisher called from down the hall.

"In here," Patrick replied. He taped a fresh bandage over the slash on Ian's shoulder blade. "That's good for now."

Fisher, Brian, Jensen, and Sal appeared in the doorway. "Since we've got our plan set, Brian thinks it would be a good time to talk to you about the other problem," Fisher said.

Patrick got to his feet. "I'll be in my room if you need me."

"Thanks," Ian said, but his gaze was on Sal.

Fisher took Patrick's hand and led him out of the room.

Patrick could tell by the grip Fisher had on him that he was worried, but Patrick wasn't. He was willing to try anything to free himself of his father for good. "It'll be okay."

The moment they entered their room, Fisher released Patrick's hand and moved to pull him into an embrace. "I don't like it." He pressed his lips to Patrick's forehead. "I hate that there's nothing I can do to protect you from it."

"You've protected me since the day we met," Patrick pointed out. "I'm not willing to risk your life just to be with you, so if Brian can help with that, I'm going for it."

"Yeah, about that," Brian began. "I can't remove your birthmark, but I think if we change it, it'll block the evil from being attracted to you."

"Okay. Tell me how?" Patrick was eager to get started.

Brian glanced at Fisher. "We can either cut or burn the birthmark. The important thing is to disrupt whatever spell has been placed on the members of your family. Cutting it, could be a problem because, as I told Fisher, I think it probably runs deep into the tissue. That would mean cutting deep, which isn't something we're set up to do. I think our best option is to brand the birthmark with another design. I've been looking through my chest, and I found this small cross." He produced a pendent from his pocket. "It belonged to my grandmother."

Patrick took the necklace from Brian to study it more closely. It was a pretty, filigreed cross that looked old. "Are you serious? All I have to do is burn this into my skin, and my dad won't be able to hurt me anymore?"

"He can't hurt you if he can't find you," Brian said. He tapped the cross in Patrick's palm. "Your birthmark isn't only a way for spirits to get in. It's like a tracking device for evil. I have to be honest, I'm not a hundred percent sure it'll work, but from what I've read, it should help. You still might run across spirits on occasion that recognize your ability to accept them inside of you. Just remember, a normal spirit doesn't have enough power to totally take over you, so you'll still be aware of your surroundings, and you might even have a choice as to whether or not you let them in."

"Why would I let them in?" Patrick asked.

Brian shrugged. "I think most spirits that continue to hang around the living do so because they weren't finished living their lives. You might call it being greedy, but sometimes they simply don't want to leave their loved ones."

Patrick clutched the necklace to his chest. "Okay. I want to do it."

Brian nodded as Fisher's hold on Patrick tightened. "Let's deal with vanquishing the evil fuckers outside first.

Once we know we can get you to a hospital if it's needed, we'll do it."

Patrick had nearly forgotten about the plan they'd agreed on earlier. He didn't like the idea of opening himself to Brother Callum again, but he had a feeling it was the only way.

"Okay."

Brian gestured to the necklace. "Keep that." He headed to the door. "I'm making a big breakfast at sunrise. After we eat, we'll get to work."

Patrick nodded.

Once Brian left the room, Fisher reached for the bottom of Patrick's T-shirt and pulled it up and off. "Do you need to use the restroom before we go to bed?"

"No." Patrick continued to clutch the necklace in his fist as Fisher stripped him of his clothes. He didn't protest because if he was only guaranteed one more night with Fisher, he didn't plan to waste a second of it.

CHAPTER SEVEN

Fisher surged in again. It was the fourth time in less than eight hours that he'd been inside Patrick, but he couldn't seem to get enough. His dick was starting to feel raw and no doubt Patrick's hole was feeling the same way, but neither of them wanted to stop. Still, Fisher tried to be as gentle as possible.

Fisher pulled out until only the tip of his cock remained inside and waited.

Patrick finally tore his gaze away from the point they were connected and looked up at Fisher. "What?"

"Just wanted to make sure you were still with me," Fisher confirmed, changing his angle. In his mind, Patrick was everything good in the world, and he still couldn't believe he'd found him. He captured Patrick's pouty lips between his teeth and bit playfully. Sex with Patrick was fun, exhilarating, and oh so damn good.

"Oh!" Patrick cried a moment before Fisher felt the heat of his release between them.

Yeah, Fisher liked that, too. It didn't seem to matter how many times Patrick came, he always seemed surprised by it. *Yep. Cute.* It didn't take long for Patrick's body to milk

Fisher into his own orgasm, but the intensity, especially after an entire night of coming, shocked him.

"Fuck!" Fisher bellowed as he rode out his climax.

Patrick laughed again and tried to cover Fisher's mouth. "Shhh, they'll hear us."

Fisher didn't care. He'd heard Jensen and Brian a few hours ago, so payback was a bitch. He pressed his lips against the crook of Patrick's neck and panted.

"Have you ever had sex in a swimming pool?" Patrick asked.

Fisher grinned. He was getting used to Patrick's off-the-wall questions. "Not in a pool, but I dated someone once who had a pond."

Patrick wrinkled his cute little nose. "Ponds are dirty. That couldn't have been safe."

Fisher didn't remind Patrick that they had worse things to worry about than the safety of pond water during sex. "You're so fucking cute."

"I'd rather be sexy," Patrick said with a pout.

Fisher licked Patrick's lip. "You're that, too."

"Good answer." Patrick smiled.

Fisher turned serious. "Promise me that you won't go outside the wards."

"I promise."

* * * *

Fisher could do nothing but watch as Patrick, or rather Brother Callum, walked out of the church. The plan was for Patrick to get the ghosts attention before luring them away. In order to ensure this, Ian had given Patrick a heavy cross that had once hung in the church. Ian kept his distance, staying approximately twenty yards behind him, with Gavin bringing up the rear. They'd armed Ian and Gavin with holy water even though they didn't know if it would help if the unthinkable happened.

Fisher gripped the shovel in his hand tighter. Gavin still refused to help, so they'd sent him with Ian and Patrick in case Brother Callum needed to communicate. That meant they were down a man when it came to the digging. They'd have to get the fuck in, do their job, and get out before they were detected. Unfortunately, they had no way of knowing if the evil had followed Patrick until they stepped outside the safety of the property.

"Remember, salt first, then water," Brian told Jensen, Sal, and Fisher.

"Yeah." Fisher stepped out of the church when Ian flashed the signal that Brother Callum had garnered the attention of the evil spirits.

"Go," Fisher said as he took off at full speed. Despite the warmer than usual day, they'd all opted to dress in heavy jeans, shirts, and coats. By the time they made it down the hill, sweat ran down Fisher's face and neck. He braced himself for battle as he blew past the wards to the cursed plot of ground.

Fisher set his shovel on the hard ground and stomped on it. They'd decided to start from the outside and work their way in, but after the first shovelful, he wasn't sure they'd be able to handle the task without a fucking backhoe.

"It's hard as a rock," he said.

"Yeah." Jensen continued to work, but Fisher could tell his mind was working on the problem. After a few minutes of digging, Jensen looked up from the shallow hole he'd dug. "Brian, could we pour water on the dirt to soften it?"

"We could, but it'll take time that we don't have." Brian shook the sweat from the ends of his hair as he sank the pickaxe down into the dirt. "Someone come over here and see if breaking it up like this helps." He scooted over and drove the pick into the ground repeatedly, breaking the soil into clods.

Fisher continued where he was, but each drive of his boot heel against the shovel sent stinging pain up his injured leg. He flicked a glance toward the church, hating that Patrick was out of eyesight.

"Let me in there," Brian said, nudging Fisher's hip.

Without breaking stride, Fisher moved to a spot of ground Brian had already broken apart. "How far down do you think?"

"Hard to say. If the ground was hard, like it is now, I can't imagine too far down. Although it was years ago, so the bones could've settled some with the elements." Brian moved closer toward the center of the circle as they all continued to dig.

Fisher had a trench about four-foot-long and two-foot-deep and two-foot-wide when it happened.

"Got something," Jensen called.

Fisher stared over to find Jensen hadn't gone as deep as he'd gone. Either the men were buried at different depths or the monks dug one hole and dumped them all in it together. He prayed that was the case.

Fisher moved to Jensen's side of the circle. "You think they're all together?"

Brian shrugged. "No way to know unless we dig up the whole thing, but the more we can uncover quickly, the better our chances with the remaining spirits."

Fisher uncovered more bones. "Don't know if it's the same guy or not, but I've got a skull."

"Got one over here, too," Sal said from the opposite side of Jensen.

"Okay. That's at least two of them then." Brian sank the pick into the ground again. "I'm not sure whether to vanquish them as we uncover them or wait until we have all of 'em because once we start, the others will be pulled back here."

Fisher started to answer, but was stopped when the sound of ripping fabric heralded a searing pain to his lower back. He automatically swung the shovel around, nearly hitting Jensen in the process. "They're here."

"Shit!" Jensen started to dig faster along with Sal and Brian when Fisher was knocked off his feet. "We've got to do it now," he warned. There were four of them, surely they could handle two spirits until the other two skeletons were uncovered.

"Sal, hand me that salt," Brian said, retrieving one of the watering cans that he'd filled with holy water.

Fisher was held to the ground by unseen hands as Brian sprinkled a handful of salt over the two partially uncovered skeletons. "Fuck!" Fisher used his hands to dig. The hard soil scraped against his knuckles and fingertips, but he didn't care. His back felt like it was on fire, and from the grunts coming from Sal, he wasn't the only one under attack.

The sound of breaking bone filled the air just before Jensen screamed and dropped his shovel.

Brian started to go to Jensen, but stopped, shook his head, and continued the ritual. He chanted in Latin while he sprinkled the water over the bones.

In an instant, the pressure on Fisher's back disappeared. He wasted no time getting to his feet as the air around them seemed to grow even heavier. Tossing the shovel to the side, he grabbed the pickaxe. He pushed down the need to help his friends and tore through the earth—searching.

When Fisher hit something hard, he lifted the pick to find he'd caught himself a skull. "Brian!" he yelled. He tossed the skull to the ground next to Brian before going back to find the rest of it.

Bleeding from a cut down the side of his face, Sal suddenly jerked, turned in a circle with his hands up ready to fight and paused. "I think it's gone." He wiped the blood with his coat sleeve before reaching for the shovel he'd dropped during the fight.

Fisher heard his name and glanced up to see Ian running down the hill with a look of horror on his face. Patrick. "Something's wrong."

"Go," Jensen urged. "We'll handle this."

Fisher glanced at Jensen and was sickened to see the sharp jagged edge of bone sticking out of Jensen's left forearm. Like Fisher had done earlier, Jensen had ditched the shovel and was using his good hand to dig.

"Go," Jensen said again.

Fisher dropped the pick and took off toward Ian. He was surprised when he didn't meet resistance as he crossed through the wards and back to safety. "What's happened?"

Panting, Ian stopped running long enough to turn around and head back in the direction he'd come. "We heard Jensen scream, then Patrick launched himself over the property line."

Fisher pushed through the pain in his back and leg and picked up speed. "What the fuck is Brother Callum thinking?"

"That's the thing. It wasn't Callum; it was Patrick," Ian gasped. "Before he crossed over, he said it needed to end, in *English*."

Fuck. Fisher crested the hill and got his first look at Patrick. Thin tendrils of smoke rose from the ground around Patrick, reminding Fisher of the scene in Sal's flower garden.

"Patrick!" Fisher yelled as he neared the property line.

"Don't." Patrick put his hands up to stop Fisher. "I think I can hold him off long enough for Brian to vanquish him."

Fisher took in the melting soles of Patrick's sneakers and the dying grass all around him. After the soil had turned scorching hot in the flower garden, Patrick hadn't shown any signs of being burned, but Fisher wasn't willing to take the chance again. He braced for the pain he knew would come. The second Fisher crossed the ward, it felt like he was walking on hot coals, but instead of coming after him, it was Patrick who was knocked off his feet.

"You can't have him!" Fisher howled as he reached for Patrick. He tried in vain to lift the man he loved, but unseen hands seemed to hold Patrick in place. "Take me!" he yelled, striking out against his ghostly enemy.

"Get out," Patrick panted. "I can't hold him off much longer."

Fisher didn't like the resigned tone of Patrick's weakening voice. "No." He couldn't give up. The plan was to vanquish the evil surrounding the church and abbey, then remove the birthmark. *Fuck.* He slammed his fist against his knee and the diamond on his ring sparkled in the sunlight. An idea came to him. He didn't know where the cross pendent was that Brian had given Patrick, but Brian had said the birthmark needed to change.

"Hang on, babe," Fisher said as he moved to rip the shoe from Patrick's foot.

The moment the birthmark was exposed, Fisher was tossed through the air away from Patrick. He landed on his side and felt the snap of one or more of his ribs as the scorching dirt seemed to burn its way through his clothes.

"No!" Fisher screamed as what felt like talons scored his body while he scrambled back to Patrick. "You can't have him." He pressed his fist to the ground and cried out when the skin on his hand blistered. "He's mine. He lifted his hand and pressed his signet ring against the birthmark. "I'm claiming him!"

All at once, the ground under him cooled, and despite the smell of burned flesh in the air, Fisher knew they'd won. He released his hold on Patrick's foot and rolled to his back.

"Fisher." Patrick moved to kneel at Fisher's side. "Stay with me." He cupped Fisher's cheek as Fisher struggled to keep his eyes open.

"You're free," Fisher mumbled. He had no idea how bad his injuries were, but he knew they wouldn't be fixed with Super Glue. He tried to concentrate on Patrick's beautiful blue eyes. "Call the WPU. I still have friends who owe me," he managed to get out before his world went dark.

EPILOGUE

One Year Later

"Yeah, we're doing good," Fisher said into the phone. "Patrick loves the new house."

"That's great," Jensen replied. "Brian wants to know if you two are going to make it out for Christmas."

Fisher looked out the large picture window and scanned the yard for Patrick. "Why don't you guys come here? You haven't seen the house yet, and I don't like taking Patrick to places I'm unsure about." He smiled at Patrick's animated conversation with himself. "Besides, I'm not sure how Patrick would feel about leaving his new pals."

"Pals? As in plural?" Jensen asked.

"Yeah. Gracie helps him with the gardening, and Phillip's currently teaching him how to make birdhouses." Fisher shook his head. Brian had been right. The change to the birthmark had made all the difference in the world. Although Patrick was still open to visiting spirits, they weren't attracted to him as they'd once been. Instead, it seemed to be Patrick's choice who he let in, and, according to Patrick, he was only sharing his body now instead of being totally consumed by the spirits. That meant Patrick would often engage in conversation with himself while sharing his body. Fisher only wished Patrick would run across the spirit of a chef because his partner couldn't cook for shit.

"I'll talk to Brian and let you know," Jensen said. "I've never been to Vancouver Island, so it might be nice to get away from the snow in December."

"It's gorgeous. Who knows, maybe you'll decide to give up the shop and move here." Fisher would love to have his friends close, but he understood why they all lived where they did. Jensen and Brian owned a bookstore that had once belonged to Brian's grandfather, and Sal and Ian were still back in France. Ian had left the church restoration to Gavin and had been using his considerable talents to build a ten-foot high stone wall around Sal's property. Fisher still wasn't sure why Sal needed the wall, but he had a feeling it was Sal's way of keeping Ian close.

"I doubt it," Jensen said, interrupting Fisher's thoughts. "Brian's pretty attached to this old place. He says he can still feel his grandfather walking around in the book stacks."

At one time, the thought of welcoming ghosts into his everyday life would have put Fisher right off, but he'd learned through Patrick that not all spirits were bad. Well, except for Walter. That horny little fucker continually tried to sneak his way into the bedroom Fisher shared with Patrick.

"I'd better let you go. Patrick and Phillip are arguing over paint colors, and I don't see it ending well for Patrick's new clothes."

Jensen chuckled. "All right. I'll talk to Brian and call you back later."

"Later," Fisher said before hanging up. He shoved the phone into his pocket as he slid open the glass door that led to the covered deck. The small bungalow hadn't had one when they'd purchased it, but Patrick had insisted they build one, and since Fisher had yet to find anything he could deny the man he loved, he built a big fucking deck.

"Why don't you take a break and come up here. We'll have a glass of wine and a cuddle before we go to dinner," Fisher suggested.

Patrick mumbled to himself before Fisher saw the customary jerk that meant Phillip had released him. "Sounds good," Patrick replied as he turned away from the still unpainted birdhouse to join Fisher on the deck.

"What were you arguing with Phillip over?" Fisher poured a glass before handing it to Patrick.

"He wants to paint the birdhouse gray and blue like this place, but I told him that would look stupid unless the birdhouse actually looked like this house." Patrick shrugged. "I think we settled on white with blue trim."

After filling his own glass, Fisher joined Patrick on their favorite round lounger. "Sounds like a good choice." He lifted his arm so Patrick could curl around him. "I talked to Jensen."

Patrick stopped kissing Fisher's neck long enough to reply. "Yeah? How are they?"

"Good. They invited us to their place for Christmas, but I told Jensen they should come here instead."

"Why?"

"Better the ghosts you know than the ones you don't," Fisher reminded Patrick.

Patrick scraped Fisher's goatee with his teeth. "Call him back and tell him we'll come. There's something I'd like to do for Brian."

"What do you want to do for Brian?" Fisher captured Patrick's mouth in a deep kiss before pulling back.

"I've been trying to think of a way to pay Brian and Jensen back for what they did for me, and I think I want to give Brian the gift of his grandfather for a few hours."

Fisher shook his head. It was one thing for the friendly spirits who lived on the island to possess Patrick for a few hours of building or gardening, but Fisher didn't know enough about Brian's grandfather or what kind of spirits hung around him. "I don't think he expects you to do something that drastic."

"Maybe not, but he told me he wishes his granddad could've met Jensen. He's done so much for me, and this is the one thing I can do for him that no one else can. At least no one we know.

Fisher understood Patrick's need to give back to Brian and Jensen for their help, but he still didn't like it. "We'll discuss it later," he said, guiding Patrick's hand down to the fly of his uniform pants. One of his favorite ways to wind down after a long day at the Oak Bay Police Department was to fool around with Patrick in the lounger.

Patrick unzipped Fisher's uniform pants before sliding his hand inside.

Fisher rested his head back on the cushion and watched as Patrick scooted down. "You going to suck me, babe?"

Patrick nodded before licking the tip of Fisher's erection.

Fisher found it hard to keep his eyes open when Patrick expertly took his entire length down his throat, but he loved watching Patrick pleasure him. He threaded his fingers through Patrick's black silky curls and groaned. "Fuck, baby."

Patrick pulled back and swirled his tongue around the sensitive head.

Fisher thrust his hips, plunging his cock deep into Patrick's mouth.

Patrick squeezed Fisher's balls as he bobbed up and down on his shaft.

Damn. Fisher grabbed the back of Patrick's head and held him down while he came. In the beginning of their relationship, Fisher had been embarrassed on more than one occasion when he'd come so quickly with Patrick's mouth on his dick, but that was before he'd discovered how much it turned Patrick on to see him lose control.

He released his hold and grinned at Patrick. "Perfect."

Patrick started to smile but jerked his attention to the sliding glass door before his grin was fully formed. "Walter!" he admonished. "Get lost."

Fisher chuckled. "Seems you're not the only one who wants my cock."

"Yeah, but I'm the only one you've claimed," Patrick replied with a huff.

Fisher gathered Patrick in his arms. "Yeah, baby, I've claimed you."

"And will you claim me again later tonight?" Patrick asked.

"Tonight, tomorrow night and every night after that.

THE END

TRADEMARK ACKNOWLEDGEMENT

The author acknowledges the trademark status and trademark owners of the following wordmarks mentioned in this work of fiction:

McDonalds: McDonalds

Coke: The Coca-Cola Company

Walmart: Wal-Mart Stores, Inc.

Super Glue: Super Glue Corporation

CAROL LYNNE

An avid reader for years, Carol Lynne decided one day to write her own brand of erotic romance. Carol juggles her time between being a full-time mother and a full-time writer. These days, you can usually find Carol nestled in her favorite chair writing steamy love scenes with a huge mug of coffee at her side.

ALSO BY
CAROL LYNNE

Printed by BoD™in Norderstedt, Germany